THE
ICE
IN
THE
BEDROOM

P. G. Wodehouse

SIMON AND SCHUSTER

New York • 1961

LIBRARY OF CONGRESS CATALOG CARD NUMBER: 61-5849

MANUFACTURED IN THE UNITED STATES OF AMERICA
BY AMERICAN BOOK—STRATFORD PRESS, INC., N. Y.

THE
ICE
IN
THE
BEDROOM

1.

Feeding his rabbits in the garden of his residence, The Nook, his humane practice at the start of each new day, Mr. Cornelius, the house agent of Valley Fields, seemed to sense a presence. He had the feeling that he was not alone. Nor was he. A lissome form had draped itself over the fence which divided his domain from that of Peacehaven next door, its lips attached to a long cigarette holder.

"Ah, Mr. Widgeon," he said. "Good morning."

With its trim gardens and tree-shaded roads, Valley Fields, that delectable suburb to the southeast of London, always presents a pleasing spectacle on a fine day in June, and each of these two householders in his individual way contributed his mite to the glamour of the local scene.

Mr. Cornelius had a long white beard which gave him something of the dignity of a Druid priest, and the young man he had addressed as Widgeon might have stepped straight out of the advertisement columns of one of the glossier and more expensive magazines. The face as clean-cut as that of any Adonis depicted wearing somebody's summer suitings for the discriminating man, the shoes just right, the socks just right, the shirt and Drones Club tie just right. Criticisms had been made from time to time of Freddie Widgeon's intelligence, notably by his uncle Lord Blicester and by Mr. Shoesmith, the solicitor, in whose office he was employed, but nobody—not even Oofy Prosser of the Drones, whom he often annoyed a good deal—had ever been able to find anything to cavil at in his outer crust.

"Lovely weather," said Mr. Cornelius.

"Just like mother makes," assented Freddie, as sunny to all appearances as the skies above. "Cigarette?"

"No, thank you. I do not smoke."

"What, never?"

"I gave it up many years ago. Doctors say it is injurious to the health."

"Doctors are asses. They don't know a good thing when they see one. How *do* you pass the long evenings?"

"I work on my history of Valley Fields."

"You're writing a history of Valley Fields?"

"I have been engaged on it for a considerable time. A labor of love."

"You like Valley Fields?"

"I love it, Mr. Widgeon. I was born in Valley Fields, I went to school in Valley Fields, I have lived all my life in Valley Fields, and I shall end my days here. I make a modest competence—"

"Mine's a stinker."

"—and I am content with it. I have my house, my garden, my wife, my flowers, my rabbits. I ask nothing more."

Freddie chafed a little. His views on suburban life differed radically from those the other had expressed, and this enthusiasm jarred on him.

"Yes, that's all right for you," he said. "You're a happy carefree house agent. I'm a wage slave in a solicitor's firm, as near to being an office boy as makes no matter. Ever see a caged eagle?"

Oddly enough, Mr. Cornelius had not. He did not get around much.

"Me," said Freddie, tapping his chest. He frowned. He was thinking of the dastardly conduct of his uncle Lord Blicester, who, on the shallow pretext that a young man ought to be earning his living and making something of himself, had stopped his allowance and shoved him into the beastly legal zoo over which Mr. Shoesmith presided. He thrust the distasteful subject from his mind and turned to pleasanter topics.

"I see you're lushing up the dumb chums."

"Always at this hour."

"What's on the menu?"

"The little fellows get their lettuce."

"They couldn't do better. Rich in vitamins and puts hair on the chest." He studied the breakfasters in silence for a moment. "Ever notice how a rabbit's nose sort of twitches? I know a girl whose nose does that when she gets excited."

"A resident of Valley Fields?" said Mr. Cornelius, searching in his mind for nose-twitchers of the suburb's younger set.

"No, she lives down in Sussex at a place called Loose Chippings."

"Ah," said Mr. Cornelius, with the gentle pity he always felt for people who did not live in Valley Fields.

"She's got a job there. She's secretary to a woman called Yorke, who writes books and things."

Mr. Cornelius started as if, mistaking him for a leaf of lettuce, one of the rabbits had bitten him.

"Not Leila Yorke the novelist?"

"That's the one. Ever sample her stuff?"

A devout look had come into the house agent's face. His beard waggled emotionally.

"She is my favorite author. I read and reread every word she writes."

"Sooner you than me. I dipped into one of her products once, misled by the title into supposing it to be a spine-freezer, and gave up the unequal struggle in the middle of Chapter Three. Slush of the worst description it seemed to me."

"Oh, Mr. Widgeon, no!"

"You don't see eye to eye?"

"I certainly do not. To me Leila Yorke plumbs the depths of human nature and lays bare the heart of woman as if with a scalpel."

"What a beastly idea! It sounds like let-me-tell-you-about-my-operation. Well, have it your own way. If hers are the sort of books you like to curl up with, go to it and best of luck. What were we talking about before we got off on to the Yorke subject? Oh yes, about me being a caged eagle. That's what I am, Cornelius, and I don't like it. The role revolts me. I want to slide out of it. Shall I tell you how a caged eagle slides out of being a caged eagle?"

"Do, Mr. Widgeon."

"It gets hold of a bit of money, and that's what I'm going to do. I want the stuff quick and plenty of it. I want people to nudge each other in the street as I pass and whisper, 'See that fellow in the fur coat? Widgeon, the millionaire.' I want to wear bank notes next to my skin winter and summer, ten-pound ones in the chilly months, changing to fivers as the weather gets warmer."

It is always difficult to be certain when a man as densely bearded as Mr. Cornelius is pursing his lips, but something of the sort seemed to be going on inside the undergrowth that masked him from the world. It was plain that he thought these aspirations sordid and distasteful.

There was an unspoken Tut-tut in his voice as he said, "But does money bring happiness, Mr. Widgeon?"

"I'll say!"

"The rich have their troubles."

"Name three."

"I was thinking of my brother Charles."

"Is he rich?"

"Extremely. He left England under a cloud, I regret to say, many years ago, and went to America, where he has done well. In the last letter I received from him he said he had an apartment on Park Avenue, which I gather is a very respectable quarter of New York, a house on Long Island, another in Florida, a private airplane and a yacht. I have always felt sorry for Charles."

"Why's that?"

"He does not live in Valley Fields," said Mr. Cornelius simply. He brooded for a moment on his brother's hard lot. "No," he continued, "the wealthy are not to be envied. Life must be a constant anxiety for them. Look at your friend Mr. Prosser, of whom you were speaking to me the other day."

This puzzled Freddie.

"Old Oofy? What's he got to worry him? Apart, of course, from being married to Shoesmith's daughter and having to call Shoesmith 'Daddy'?"

It seemed to Mr. Cornelius that his young friend must

have a very short memory. It was only the day before yesterday that they had been discussing the tragedy which had befallen the Prosser home.

"You told me that Mrs. Prosser had been robbed of jewelry worth many thousands of pounds."

Freddie's face cleared.

"Oh, that? Yes, someone got away with her bit of ice all right. The maid, they think it must have been, because when the alarm was raised and the cops charged in, they found she had gone without a cry. But bless your kind old heart, Cornelius, Oofy doesn't care. It happened more than a month ago, and the last time I saw him he was as blithe as a bird. He'd got the insurance money."

"Nevertheless, occurrences of that nature are very unpleasant, and they happen only to the rich."

It was Freddie's opinion that the house agent was talking through his hat. He did not say so, for the other's white hair protected him, but his manner, as he spoke, was very firm.

"Listen, my dear old lettuce-distributor," he said, "I see what you mean, and your reasoning is specious, if that's the word, but I still stick to it that what you need in this world is cash, and that is why you may have noticed that I've been looking a bit more cheerful these last days. The luck of the Widgeons has turned, and affluence stares me in the eyeball."

"Indeed?"

"I assure you. For the first time in years Frederick Fotheringay Widgeon is sitting on top of the world with a rainbow round his shoulder. You could put it in a nutshell by saying that Moab is my washpot and over wherever-it-was will I cast my shoe, as the fellow said, though what casting shoes has got to do with it is more than I can tell you. Do you know a chap called Thomas G. Molloy? American bloke. Lives at Castlewood next door to me on the other side."

"Yes, I am acquainted with Mr. Molloy. I saw him only yesterday, when he came to my office to give me the keys."

Freddie could make nothing of this.

"What did he want to give you keys for? Your birthday or something?"

"The keys of the house. He has left Castlewood."

"What?"

"Yes, Castlewood is vacant once more. But I anticipate very little difficulty in disposing of it," said Mr. Cornelius (nearly adding from force of habit, "A most desirable property, tastefully furnished throughout and standing in parklike grounds extending to upwards of a quarter of an acre"). "There is a great demand for that type of house."

Freddie was still perplexed. Saddened, too, for in his vanished neighbor he felt he had lost a friend. Thomas G. Molloy's rich personality had made a strong appeal to him.

"But I thought Molloy owned Castlewood."

"Oh no, he merely occupied it on a short lease. These three houses—Castlewood, Peacehaven and The Nook—are the property of a Mr. Keggs, who has lived at Castlewood for many years. It was sublet to Mr. Molloy when Mr. Keggs went off on one of those round-the-world cruises. He came into a great deal of money recently and felt he could afford the trip. Though why anyone living in Valley Fields should want to leave it and go gadding about, I cannot imagine. But you were speaking of Mr. Molloy. Why did you mention him?"

"Because it is he who has brought these roses to my cheeks. Entirely owing to that bighearted philanthropist, I shall very shortly be in a position to strike off the shackles of Shoesmith, Shoesmith, Shoesmith and Shoesmith. I thought I was in for a life sentence in the Shoesmith snake pit, and the prospect appalled me. And then Molloy came along. But I'm getting ahead of my story. All back to Chapter One, when I got that letter from Boddington. Pal of mine in Kenya," Freddie explained. "Runs a coffee ranch or whatever you call it out there. He wrote to me and asked if I'd like to take a small interest in it and come and join the gang. Well, of course I was all for it. Nothing could be more up my street. Are you familiar with the expression 'the great open spaces'?"

Mr. Cornelius said he was. Leila Yorke's heroes, he said, frequently made for the great open spaces when a misunderstanding had caused a rift between them and the girls they loved.

"Those are what I've always yearned for, and I understand the spaces in Kenya are about as open as they come. I don't quite know how you set about growing coffee, but one soon picks these things up. I am convinced that, given a spade and a watering can and shown the way to the bushes, it will not be long before I electrify the industry, raising a sensational bean. Kenya ho! is the slogan. That's where you get the rich, full life."

"Kenya is a long way off."

"Part of its charm."

"I would not care to go so far from Valley Fields myself."

"The farther the better, in my opinion. I can take Valley Fields or leave it alone."

These words, bordering to his mind closely on blasphemy, caused Mr. Cornelius to wince. He turned away and offered a portion of lettuce to the third rabbit on the right in rather a marked manner.

"So you are accepting your friend's offer?" he said, when he had recovered himself.

"If he'll hold it open for a while. Everything turns on

that. You see, as always when these good things come your way, there's a catch. I have to chip in with three thousand quid as a sort of entrance fee, and I don't mind telling you that when I read that passage in the Boddington communiqué, I reeled and might have fallen, had I not been sitting down at the time. Because I don't need to tell you, Cornelius, that three thousand quid is heavy sugar."

"You mean that your funds were insufficient to meet this condition?"

"Very far short of sweetening the kitty. All I had in the world was a measly thousand, left me by a godmother."

"Unfortunate."

"Most. I asked an uncle of mine for a temporary loan of the sum I needed, and all he said was 'What, what, what? Absurd. Preposterous. Couldn't think of it,' which, as you will readily agree, left no avenue open for a peaceful settlement. Oofy Prosser, too, declined to be my banker, as did my banker, and I was just about to write the whole thing off as a washout, when suddenly there was a fanfare of angel trumpets and Molloy descended from heaven, the sun shining on his wings. We got talking, I revealed my predicament, and he waved his magic wand and solved all my problems. In return for my thousand quid he let me have some very valuable oil stock which he happened to have in his possession."

"Good gracious!"

"I put it even more strongly."

"What oil stock?"

"Silver River it's called, and pretty soon England will be ringing with its name. He says it's going up and up and up, the sky the only limit."

"But was it not a little rash to invest all your capital in a speculative concern?"

"Good heavens, I leaped at the chance like a jumping

bean. And it isn't speculative. Molloy stressed that. It's absolutely gilt-edged. He assures me I shall be able to sell my holdings for at least ten thousand in less than a month."

"Strange that he should have parted with anything so valuable."

"He explained that. He said he liked my face. He said I reminded him of a nephew of his on whom he had always looked as a son, who handed in his dinner pail some years ago. Double pneumonia. Very sad."

"Oh, dear!"

"Why do you say 'Oh, dear!'?"

But Mr. Cornelius's reasons for uttering this observation were not divulged, for even as he spoke Freddie had happened to glance at his wrist watch, and what he saw there shook him from stem to stern.

"Good Lord, is that the time?" he gasped. "I'll miss that ruddy train again!"

He sped off, and Mr. Cornelius looked after him with a thoughtful eye. If youth but knew, he seemed to be saying to himself. He had not been favorably impressed by Thomas G. Molloy, late of Castlewood, who, possibly because he, Mr. Cornelius, reminded him, Mr. Molloy, of a goat he had been fond of as a child, had tried to sell him, too, a block of stock in this same Silver River Oil and Refinery Corporation.

With a sigh he picked up a leaf of lettuce and went on feeding his rabbits.

2.

All season-ticket holders who live in the suburbs run like
the wind, and Freddie had long established himself as one
of Valley Fields's most notable performers on the flat, but
today, though he clipped a matter of three seconds off his
previous record for the Peacehaven-to-station course, he
had given the 8:45 too long a start and had to wait for the
9:06. It was consequently with some trepidation that he
entered the Shoesmith premises, a trepidation which the
cold gray eye of Mr. Jervis, the head clerk, did nothing to
allay. He had no need to look into a crystal ball to predict
that there might be a distressing interview with Mr. Shoesmith in the near future. From their initial meeting and
from meetings that had taken place subsequently he had

been able to gather that the big shot was a stickler for punctuality on the part of the office force.

But it was not this thought that was clouding his brow as he sat at the desk at which he gave his daily impersonation of a caged eagle. He did not enjoy those chats with Mr. Shoesmith, whose forte was dry sarcasm, very wounding to the feelings, but custom had inured him to them and he was able now to take them with a philosophical fortitude. The reason melancholy marked him for its own was that he was thinking of Sally Foster.

If Mr. Cornelius had not been so intent at the moment on seeing to it that the personnel of his hutch got their proper supply of vitamins, he might have observed that at the mention of the girl whose nose twitched like a rabbit's a quick spasm of pain had flitted across the young man's face. It had been only a passing twinge, gone almost immediately, for the Widgeons could wear the mask, but it had been there. He had rashly allowed himself to be reminded of Sally Foster, and whenever that happened it was as though he had bitten on a sensitive tooth.

There had been a time, and not so long ago, when he and Sally had been closer than the paper on the wall— everything as smooth as dammit, each thinking the other the biggest thing since sliced bread and not a cloud on the horizon. And then, just because she had found him kissing that dumb brick of a Bunting girl at that cocktail party— the merest civil gesture, as he had tried to explain, due entirely to the fact that he had run out of conversation and felt that he had to do something to keep things going— she had blown a gasket and forbidden the banns. Take back your mink, take back your pearls, she would no doubt have said, if his finances had ever run to giving her mink and pearls. What she had actually returned to him by district messenger boy had been a bundle of letters, half a bottle of Arpege and five signed photographs.

Yes, he had lost her. And—which made it all the more bitter—here he was in London, chained to the spot without a chance of getting away till his annual holiday in November, while she was down in Sussex at Claines Hall, Loose Chippings. Not an earthly, in short, of being able to get to her and do a little quick talking, a thing he knew himself to be good at, and persuading her to forget and forgive. It is not too much to say that at the moment when Elsa Bingley, Mr. Shoesmith's secretary, touched him on the shoulder, bringing him out of the wreck of his hopes and dreams with a jerk, Frederick Widgeon was plumbing the depths.

"His nibs wants to see you, Freddie," said Elsa Bingley, and he nodded a somber nod. He had rather thought that this might happen.

In the inner lair where he lurked during business hours, Mr. Shoesmith was talking to his daughter Mrs. Myrtle Prosser, who had looked in for a chat as she did sometimes—too often, in Mr. Shoesmith's opinion, for he disliked having to give up his valuable time to someone to whom he could not send in a bill. At the mention of Freddie's name Myrtle showed a mild interest.

"Widgeon?" she said. "Is that Freddie Widgeon?"

"I believe his name is Frederick. You know him?"

"He's a sort of friend of Alexander's. He comes to dinner sometimes when we need an extra man. I didn't know he worked here."

"It is a point on which I am somewhat doubtful myself," said Mr. Shoesmith. "Much depends on what interpretation you place on the word *work*. To oblige his uncle Lord Blicester, whose affairs have been in my hands for many years, I took him into my employment and he arrives in the morning and leaves in the evening, but apart from a certain rudimentary skill in watching the clock, probably instinctive, I would describe him as essentially a lily of the field. Ah, Mr. Widgeon."

The lily of the field of whom he was speaking had entered, and, seeing Myrtle, had swayed a little on his stem. This daughter of Mr. Shoesmith who had married Alexander ("Oofy") Prosser—a thing not many girls would have cared to do—was a young woman of considerable but extremely severe beauty. She did not resemble her father, who looked like a cassowary, but suggested rather one of those engravings of the mistresses of Bourbon kings which make one feel that the monarchs who selected them must have been men of iron, impervious to fear, or else short-sighted. She always scared Freddie to the marrow. With most of the other sex he was on easy terms—too easy was the view of his late fiancée—but the moon of Oofy Prosser's delight never failed to give him an uncomfortable feeling in the pit of the stomach and the illusion that his hands and feet had swelled unpleasantly.

"Oh, hullo, Mrs. Oofy," he said, recovering his equilibrium. "Good morning."

"Good morning."

"Going strong?"

"I am quite well, thank you."

"Oofy going strong?"

"Alexander, too, is quite well."

"Fine. He was telling me about those bits and pieces of yours."

"I beg your pardon?"

"Your jewelry. Getting stolen and all that."

"Oh, yes."

"Bad show."

"Very."

"But you've got the insurance money, he tells me."

"Yes."

"Good show."

Mr. Shoesmith broke in on these intellectual exchanges. He was not a man who suffered Freddie Widgeon gladly, considering him what in an earlier age would have been called a popinjay. Their souls were not attuned, as Freddie would have been the first to concede, though with the proviso that it was very doubtful if his employer had a soul. He had been serving under his banner for some six months now, and not a sign of one so far.

"I wonder if you could spare me your attention for a moment, Mr. Widgeon."

By standing on one leg and allowing his lower jaw to droop Freddie indicated that he would be delighted to do so.

"You have no objection to me talking shop for a little while?"

None whatever, Freddie indicated by standing on the other leg.

"Mr. Jervis tells me you were late again this morning."

"Er—yes."

"This frequently happens."

"Yes, sir. These suburban trains, you know."

"Well, no doubt we should consider ourselves fortunate that we are given at least some of your time, but I must ask you in future to try to synchronize your arrival at the office with that of the rest of the staff. We aim as far as possible at the communal dead heat."

"Yes, sir."

"So do your best, Mr. Widgeon, even if it means taking an earlier suburban train."

"Yes, sir."

"Or two suburban trains. You see, when you fail to appear, we become nervous and jumpy. Some accident must have occurred, we whisper to each other, and these gruesome speculations, so bad for office morale, continue until some clear thinker like Mr. Jervis points out that it would be a far greater accident if you were ever on time. However, that was not primarily what I wished to see you about. If you can tear yourself away from your desk this afternoon, I should like to engage your services for a confidential mission."

"Yes, sir."

"I have here some documents requiring the signature of Miss Leila Yorke, whose name will probably be familiar to you. Take them to her, if you will be kind enough, after lunch. Her address is Claines Hall, Loose Chippings, Sussex. You book your ticket at Victoria and alight at Loose Chippings station. The Hall is within an easy walk. Have I made myself clear?"

"Yes, sir."

"Splendid," said Mr. Shoesmith. "Thank you, Mr. Widgeon, that is all."

Eminent solicitors very seldom pay much attention to the muscular twitchings of the minor members of their staff, and Mr. Shoesmith, issuing these instructions, did not observe that at the mention of Claines Hall, Loose Chippings, Sussex, his young subordinate had started; but he had, and violently. His master's voice had affected him like a powerful electric shock, causing the eyeballs to rotate and everything for an instant to go black. It was only by the exercise of the greatest care that he was able to remove himself from the presence without tripping over his feet, so profoundly had the thought that he was going to see Sally again stirred him. For the rest of the morning and all through his frugal lunch at the Drones he brooded tensely on the situation which had arisen, running, it would not be too much to say, the gamut of the emotions.

At the outset he had been all joy and effervescence, feeling that out of a blue sky Fate had handed him the most stupendous bit of goose and that all was for the best in this best of all possible worlds, but as the time went by doubts began to creep in. Was this, he found himself asking himself, a good show or a bad show? Would seeing Sally alleviate that yearning feeling which so often darkened his days, or—let's face it—would he merely be twisting the knife in the wound, as the expression was? The question was a very moot one, and it is not surprising that those of his clubmates who threw lumps of sugar at him during the meal commented on his lack of sparkle and responsiveness.

On the whole, though it was a close thing, he was inclined to think that the show's goodness outweighed its badness. Agony, of course, to see her face to face and think of what might have been, but on the other hand there was always the chance that Time the great healer might have been doing its stuff, softening her heart and causing better counsels to prevail.

His mood, in consequence, as he made his way to Victoria and bought his ticket, was on the whole optimistic. Many a girl, he told himself, who in the heat of the moment has handed her loved one the pink slip, finds after thinking it over in the privacy of her chamber in the course of sleepless nights that what she supposed to be a sound, rational move was in reality the floater of a lifetime. Remorse, in short, supervenes, and when the rejected one suddenly pops up out of a trap before her, her eyes widen, her nose twitches, her lips part, she cries "Oh, Freddie darling!" and flings herself into his arms, and all is gas and gaiters again.

The day was Friday, never a good day for traveling, and

the congestion in all parts of the station had extended itself to the train for Loose Chippings. It bulged at every seam with human sardines. Faced with a choice between compartments filled with outsize adults and those where the adults were more streamlined but were accompanied by children, he chose one of the former. Only standing room remained in the little Black Hole of Calcutta which he had selected, so he stood, and from this elevation was able to see his fellow travelers steadily and see them whole.

There were eight of them, three men who looked like farmers, three women who looked like farmers' wives, a man in black who might have been an undertaker in a modest line of business, and over in the far corner a small, trim girl who was reading a magazine. She immediately arrested Freddie's attention. There was something about her that reminded him of Sally. Extraordinarily like Sally she was, from what he could see of her, and the next moment he was able to understand why there was such a resemblance.

It was Sally. She looked up from her magazine as the train started, and her eyes met his.

They were, he noted, as blue as ever, and the nose, the one that twitched like a rabbit's, still tilted slightly at the tip. The mouth was as of yore a little wide. Of the teeth he could not judge, for she was not smiling, but what he could see of her hair remained that attractive copper color he had always admired so much. Her face, in short, taking it by and large, was exactly as he remembered it from, it sometimes seemed to him, a previous existence, and at the sight of it he was conscious of an elation so pronounced that if the three farmers, the three farmers' wives and the undertaker had not been present, he would have snorted like the warhorse which, we are told, though it seems odd, used to say "Ha, ha!" among the trumpets.

3.

"Loose Chippings," chanted the porter as the train saun-
tered into the little country station, and Sally pushed her
way through the sea of legs between her and the door and
stepped down onto the platform.

She was furious, and, she considered, justly. At the cost
of much mental distress she had cast this man out of her
life because prudence told her he was irresponsible and
not to be trusted, and it was monstrous that he should
come sneaking back into it like this, reminding her that
she still loved him and reviving all the old emotions
which she had hoped she had killed long ago.

She fortified herself for the coming encounter by the
simple process of thinking of that fatal cocktail party when

the scales had fallen from her eyes and she had seen him for what he was.

She had been warned. There had been a group of young men near the door at that cocktail party, and as she had been passing them she had heard one of them utter these frightful words: "I suppose if all the girls Freddie Widgeon has been in love with were placed end to end—not that one could do it, of course—they would reach from Piccadilly Circus to Hyde Park Corner. Further than that, probably, because some of them were pretty tall."

And it was as she had been passing through the door, not wishing to sully her ears any longer, that she had come upon the Widgeon-Bunting combination linked in a close embrace on the top landing.

The recollection made her strong again. She looked at him as he stood beaming by the penny-in-the-slot machine, and an imperious desire swept over her to wipe that silly smile off his face.

"Freddie," she said, speaking from between clenched teeth, "go home!"

"Eh?"

"I told you I never wanted to see you again. Didn't you understand?"

"Well, yes, I more or less grasped that."

"Then why have you followed me here?"

Freddie stiffened. He ceased to beam. It pained him to find that he had overestimated the potentialities of Time the great healer and that the platform of Loose Chippings station was not to be the scene of a tender reconciliation, but righteous wrath overcame pain. He was deeply offended at being accused for once in his life of something of which he was not guilty. The apologetic lover became the man of ice, and he, too, spoke from between clenched teeth.

"Who's followed who where?" he said haughtily. "I'm here on business."

"*You?*"

"Yes, me. I've come to see Miss Leila Yorke. I understand she hangs out at a joint called Claines Hall. Perhaps you would be good enough to direct me there."

"I'll take you there."

"You won't object to being seen in public with one of our leading underworld characters?"

"There's no need to be so pompous."

"Yes, there is. Every need. I feel pompous. Followed you here, forsooth! You could have knocked me down with a banana skin when I saw you on that train. What were you doing in London, anyway?"

"I had to see Miss Yorke's agent about something."

"Oh, was that it? Do you often get up to London?"

"Very seldom."

"You're lucky. Lousy place. Ruddy sink of a place. No good to man or beast. Not a soul in it except blighters with brief cases and blisters in bowler hats."

"What's happened to the girls? Have they all emigrated?"

"Girls! They mean nothing in my life."

"Says you!"

"Yes, says me. Don't you believe me?"

"No, I don't. You're like the leopard."

"I'm not in the least like a leopard. What particular leopard had you in mind?"

"The one that couldn't change its spots."

"I call that a most distasteful crack."

"I'm sorry. Shall we be starting for the Hall?"

"Just as you like."

They came out into the High Street of Loose Chippings. The town's "pop," as the guidebook curtly terms it, is

4,916, and at perhaps two hundred and four of these Freddie glared bleakly as they passed on their way. He would have glared with equal bleakness at the other four thousand seven hundred and twelve, had they been there, for he was in sullen mood. Here he was, with Sally at his side, and for all the good it was doing him she might have been miles away. Aloof, that was the word he was groping for. She was distant and aloof. Not a trace of the old Sally who in happier days had been such a stupendously good egg. For all the kick she appeared to be getting out of his society, she might have been walking with an elderly uncle. Since entering the High Street she had not spoken except to direct his attention to the statue erected in the Market square to the memory of the late Anthony Briggs, J. P., for many years parliamentary representative for the local division, and if ever in Freddie's jaundiced opinion there was a ghastly statue of a potbellied baggy-trousered Gawd-help-us, this statue was that statue.

Conversation was still flagging when after leaving Loose Chippings and its pop behind and passing down a leafy lane they arrived at massive iron gates opening on a vista of shady drive, at the end of which could be seen glimpses of a Tudor mansion bathed in the afternoon sunlight.

"This is it," said Sally. "Nice place, don't you think?"

"It'll do," said Freddie, who was still in the grip of dudgeon.

"It has a moat."

"Oh, yes?"

"And a wonderful park."

"Really? La Yorke does herself well. And can afford to, of course. Oofy Prosser tells me she makes a packet with her pen. He's got a lot of money in the firm that publishes her stuff."

"I know. He was down here seeing Miss Yorke the other day. Have you met him lately?"

"Oh, yes, he's generally in at the Drones for lunch. His wife had her jewels pinched not long ago."

"So I read in the paper. Were they very valuable?"

"Worth thousands, I should think. They looked that way to me."

"You've seen them?"

"I've been to dinner once or twice with the Oofys, and she had them all on. She glittered like a chandelier."

"And they haven't got them back?"

"No."

"Too bad."

"Yes."

"It must have upset her."

"I suppose so."

Sally's heart was aching. All this formality and stiffness, as if they were strangers meeting for the first time and making conversation. Her own fault, of course, but a girl had to be sensible. If she were not, what ensued? She found herself fetching up at the end of that long line stretching from Piccadilly Circus to Hyde Park Corner. On the stage on which Frederick Widgeon strutted, she told herself, there were no female stars, just a mob of extras doing crowd work.

She forced herself to resume the conversation as they walked up the drive.

"Where are you living now, Freddie? At the old flat?"

His face, already dark, darkened still further.

"No, I couldn't afford it. My uncle stopped my allowance, and I had to move to the suburbs. I'm sharing a house with my cousin George. You remember George?"

"Dimly."

"Beefy chap with red hair. Boxed for Oxford as a heavy-weight. He's one of the local cops."

"He went into the police?"

"That's right. Said it was a darned sight better than being cooped up in an office all day, like me."

"Like you? You aren't in an office?"

"I am. A solicitor's. Shortly after we— Soon after I last saw you my foul Uncle Rodney bunged me into the firm of Shoesmith, Shoesmith, Shoesmith and Shoesmith of Lincoln's Inn Fields."

Sally, firm in her resolve to be sensible, had not planned to betray any human feeling during this painful encounter, but at these words she was unable to repress a cry of pity.

"Oh, Freddie! Not really?"

"That's what he did. He placed me in the hands of his solicitor."

"But you must hate it."

"I loathe it."

"What do you do there?"

"I'm a sort of 'Hey, you' or dogsbody like the chap in 'Old Man River.' "

"Lift that trunk?"

"Shift that bale. Exactly. Today, for instance, old Shoesmith gave me some documents to take to Leila Yorke to sign. Why he couldn't just have popped them in the post is a matter between him and his God, if any. Tomorrow I shall probably be running down the street to fetch someone a cup of coffee and the day after that sweeping out the office. I tell you, when I see George coming in off his beat with a face all bright and rosy from a health-giving day in the fresh air, while I'm pale and wan after eight hours in a stuffy office, I envy him and wish I'd had the sense to become a copper."

"How do you two manage, living all alone with nobody to look after you? Or have you a cook?"

Freddie laughed hackingly.

"You mean a chef? On our starvation wages? No, we have no chef, no butler, no first and second footmen, no head and under housemaids, and no groom of the chambers. George does the cooking, and pretty ghastly it is. But I mustn't bore you with my troubles."

"Oh, Freddie, you aren't."

"Well, I shall if I go on any longer. Change the subject, what? How do you get along with Leila Yorke?"

"Oh, splendidly. She's the top."

"In what respect?"

"In every respect."

"Not in her literary output. You must admit that she writes the most awful bilge."

"No longer."

"How do you mean, no longer?"

"She's giving up doing that sentimental stuff of hers."

"You're kidding. No more slush?"

"So she says."

"But it sells like hot cakes."

"I know."

"Then why? What's she going to do? Retire?"

"No, she's planning to write one of those stark, strong novels— You know, about the gray underworld."

"Lord love a duck! This'll be a blow to Cornelius."

"Who's he?"

"Fellow I know. He reads everything she writes."

"I wonder if he'll read her next one."

"How's it coming?"

"It hasn't started yet. She feels the surroundings at Claines Hall aren't right. She says she can't get into the mood. She wants to move somewhere where she can soak in the gray atmosphere and really get going. What's the matter?"

"Nothing."

"You sort of jumped."

"Oh, that? Touch of cramp. Has she found a place to go to yet?"

"No, she's still thinking it over."

"Ah!"

"Ah what?"

"Just Ah. Well, here we are at the old front door. What's the procedure? Do I charge in?"

"You'd better wait. I'll tell her you're here."

Sally crossed the hall, knocked on a door, went in and came out again.

"She wants you to go in."

There was a pause.

"Well, Freddie," said Sally.

"Well, Sally," said Freddie.

"I suppose this is the last time we shall meet."

"You never know."

"I think it is."

"You wouldn't care to dash in and have lunch with me one of these days?"

"Oh, Freddie, what's the use?"

"I see what you mean. Well, in that case Bung-ho about sums it up, what?"

"Yes. Goodbye, Freddie."

"Goodbye."

"Better not keep Miss Yorke waiting. She's been a little edgy since she made her great decision," said Sally, and she went off to the potting shed by the kitchen garden to have a good cry. She knew she had done the sensible thing, but that did not prevent her feeling that her heart was being torn into small pieces by a platoon of muscular wildcats, than which few experiences are less agreeable.

4.

Freddie's first sight of Mr. Cornelius' favorite novelist, author of *For True Love Only, Heather o' the Hills, Sweet Jennie Dean* and other works, had something of the effect on him of a blow between the eyes with a wet fish, causing him to rock back on his heels and blink. Going by the form book, he had expected to see a frail little spectacled wisp of a thing with a shy smile and a general suggestion of lavender and old lace. From this picture Leila Yorke in the flesh deviated quite a good deal. She was a large, hearty-looking woman in the early forties, built on the lines of Catherine of Russia, and her eyes, which were blue and bright and piercing, were obviously in no need of glasses. She wore riding breeches and was smoking a mild cigar.

"Hullo there," she said in a voice which recalled to him that of the drill sergeant at his preparatory school, a man who could crack windows with a single " 'Shun!" "You Widgeon?"

"That's right. How do you do?"

"Shoesmith phoned me that you were bringing those papers. I'll bet you left them in the train."

"No, I have them here."

"Then let's sign the blasted things and get it over with."

She scribbled her signature with the flowing pen of a woman accustomed to recording her name in autograph albums, offered him a cigar and disposed herself for conversation.

"Widgeon?" she said. "That's odd. I used to know a Rodney Widgeon once. Know him still, as a matter of fact, only he goes around under an alias these days. Calls himself Lord Blicester. Any relation?"

"My uncle."

"You don't say? You don't look like him."

"No," said Freddie, who would have hated to. There was nothing in the appearance of his Uncle Rodney that appealed to his aesthetic sense.

"Do you brim over with a nephew's love for him?"

"I wouldn't say 'brim over' exactly."

"No objection, then, to my calling him an old poop?"

"None whatever," said Freddie, warming to the woman as he seldom warmed to one of the opposite sex over the age of twenty-five. There was no question in his mind that he and Leila Yorke were twin souls. "As a matter of fact, your words are music to my ears. 'Old poop' sums him up to a nicety."

She blew a meditative smoke ring, her thoughts plainly back in the past.

"I was engaged to him once."

"Really?"

"Broke it off, though, when he started to bulge at every seam. Couldn't keep that boy off the starchy foods. I don't mind a poop being a poop, but I draw the line at a poop who looks like two poops rolled into one."

"Quite. Have you seen him lately?"

"Not for a year or so. Is he as fat as ever?"

"He came out top in the Fat Uncles contest at the Drones last summer."

"I'm not surprised. Mark you, I'd have broken the engagement any way, because soon after we plighted our troth Joe Bishop came along."

"Joe Bishop?"

"Character I subsequently married. We split up later, and I've been kicking myself ever since. Silliest thing I ever did, to let him go. You married?"

"No."

"What are you screwing up your face for?"

"Did I screw up my face?"

"I got that impression. As if in anguish."

"I'm sorry."

"Quite all right. It's your face. Well, well, it's strange to think that if Joe hadn't come into my life and your uncle had done bending and stretching exercises and learned the knack of laying off sweets, butter and potatoes, you might now be calling me Aunt Bessie."

"Leila, you mean."

"No, I don't. Leila Yorke's my pen name. I was born Elizabeth Binns. You can't write books if you're a Binns. But let's go on roasting your uncle. You don't seem very fond of him."

"Not at the moment. He has incurred my displeasure."

"How was that?"

Freddie quivered a little. He always quivered when he thought of his Uncle Rodney's black act.

"He sold me down the river to Shoesmith."

"Don't you like working for him?"

"No."

"I wouldn't myself. How is Johnny Shoesmith these days?"

Hearing the Frankenstein's monster who employed him alluded to in this fashion shook Freddie to his depths. A vision of himself calling that eminent solicitor Johnny rose before his eyes, and he shuddered strongly. It was only after some moments that he was able to reply.

"Oh, he's fizzing along."

"I've known him since we were both so high."

"Really?"

"He once kissed me behind a rhododendron bush."

Freddie started.

"Shoesmith did?"

"Yes."

"You mean Shoesmith of Shoesmith, Shoesmith, Shoesmith and Shoesmith of Lincoln's Inn Fields?"

"That's right."

"Well, I'll be a son of a— I mean, how very extraordinary!"

"Oh, he was a regular devil in those days. And look at him now. All dried up like a kippered herring and wouldn't kiss Helen of Troy if you brought her to him asleep in a chair with a sprig of mistletoe suspended over her. He'd consider it a tort or a misdemeanor or something. That's what comes of being a solicitor—it saps the vital juices. Johnny doesn't even embezzle his clients' money, which I should have thought was about the only fun a solicitor can get out of life. How long have you been working for him?"

"Six months or so."

"You haven't dried up yet."

"No."

"Well, be careful you don't. Exercise ceaseless vigilance. And talking of drying up, you're probably in need of a quick one after your journey. Care for something moist?"

"I'd love it."

"I've only got whisky, brandy, gin, beer, sherry, port, curaçao and champagne, but help yourself. Over there in the 'fridge in the corner."

"Oh, thanks. You?"

"Why, yes, I think I might. I've been feeling a little nervous and fragile these last few days. Open a bottle of champagne."

"Right," said Freddie, doing so. "Nervous and fragile?"

"Got a lot on my mind. Widgeon," said Miss Yorke, draining her beaker and extending it for a refill, "I am standing at a woman's crossroads. Do you read my stuff?"

"Well—er—what with one thing and another . . ."

"No need to apologize. One can't read everything, and no doubt you're all tied up with your Proust and Kafka. Well, for your information, it's lousy."

"Really?"

"Pure treacle. Would you call me a sentimental woman?"

"Not offhand."

"I'm not. In the ordinary give-and-take of life I'm as tough an egg as ever stepped out of the saucepan. Did my butler show you in when you arrived?"

"No. I came with your secretary, Miss Foster. I met her on the train. We—er—we know each other slightly."

"Oh, yes, I remember it was Sally who told me you were here. Well, you ought to see my butler. Haughty? The haughtiest thing you ever met. I've seen strong publishers wilt beneath his eye. And yet that man, that haughty butler, curls up like a sheet of carbon paper if I look squiggle-eyed at him. That's the sort of woman I am when I haven't a pen in my hand, but give me a ball-point and what happens? Don't keep all that champagne to yourself."

"Oh, sorry."

"And don't spill it. The prudent man doesn't waste a drop."

"It's good stuff."

"It's excellent stuff. It's what Johnny Shoesmith needs to make him realize he isn't something dug out of Tutankhamen's tomb. Where was I?"

"You were saying what happens."

"What happens when what?"

"When you get a ball-point pen in your hand."

"Oh, yes. The moment my fingers clutch it, Widgeon, a great change comes over me. I descend to depths of goo which you with your pure mind wouldn't believe possible. I write about stalwart men, strong but oh so gentle, and girls with wide gray eyes and hair the color of ripe wheat who are always having misunderstandings and going to Africa. The men, that is. The girls stay at home and marry the wrong bimbos. But there's a happy ending. The bimbos break their necks in the hunting field and the men come back in the last chapter and they and the girls get together in the twilight, and all around is the scent of English flowers and birds singing their evensong in the shrubbery. Makes me shudder to think of it."

"It sounds rather good to me. I wouldn't mind getting together with a girl in the twilight."

"No, it's kind of you to try to cheer me up, Widgeon, but I know molasses when I see it. Or is it 'them'? The critics call my stuff tripe."

"No!"

"That's what they do, they call it tripe."

"Monstrous!"

"And of course it is tripe. But I'm not going to have a bunch of inky pipsqueaks telling me so. And I'm fed to the teeth with all these smart alecks who do parodies of me, hoping to make me feel like a piece of cheese. The worm has turned, Widgeon. Do you know what I'm going to do? I'm going to write a novel that'll make their eyes pop out. What some call an important novel, and others significant. Keep that champagne circulating. Don't let it congeal."

"But can you?"

"Can I what?"

"Write an important novel."

"Of course I can. All you have to do is cut out the plot and shove in plenty of misery. I can do it on my head, once I get started. Only the hell of it is that as long as I remain at Claines Hall, Loose Chippings, I can't get started. The atmosphere here is all wrong. Butlers and moats and things popping about all over the place. I've got to get away somewhere where there's a little decent squalor."

"That's exactly what Sally Foster was saying."

"Oh, was she? Nice girl, that. She ought to marry somebody. Maybe she will before long. I think she's in love."

"You do?"

"Yes, I've an idea there's someone for whom she feels sentiments deeper and warmer than those of ordinary friendship. Well, if so, I wish her luck. Love's all right. Makes the world go round, they say. I don't know if there's anything in it. Or if there's anything in that bottle. Is there?"

"Just a drop."

"Let's have it. What were we talking about?"

"You getting away somewhere where there was a spot of squalor."

"That's right. I thought I'd be able to swing it here by going the round of the local pubs and having the peasantry bare their souls to me. Thomas Hardy stuff. Not a hope. At the end of a week all I had discovered about these sons of toil was that they were counting the days to the football season so that they could start in on their pools again. Makes one sick. No help to a woman. Why are you looking at me like a half-witted sheep?"

"Was I?"

"You were."

"I'm sorry. It's just that when Sally Foster was telling me about this new binge you were contemplating, I had an idea."

"Beginner's luck."

"I believe I've got the very spot for you. Castlewood, Mulberry Grove, Valley Fields."

"Where's that?"

"Just outside London. I doubt if you could find a grayer locality. The man who lives next door to me keeps rabbits."

"Oh, you live in Valley Fields?"

"That's right. Castlewood's next door to me on the other side. And it's vacant at the moment and fully furnished. You could move in tomorrow. Shall I fix you up with the rabbit fancier? He's the house agent."

"H'm."

"Don't say 'H'm'!"

"I wonder."

"I wouldn't. Strike while the iron's hot is my advice."

But Miss Yorke insisted on relapsing into thought, and Freddie scanned her pensive face anxiously. On her decision so much depended. For he was convinced that if he could only get Sally on the other side of the garden fence that divided Peacehaven from Castlewood, he would soon be able to alter the present trend of her thoughts with the burning words and melting looks he knew he had at his disposal. He had lived in the suburbs long enough to be aware that the preliminaries of seventy per cent of the marriages that occurred there had been arranged over garden fences.

Leila Yorke came out of her reverie.

"I hadn't thought of the suburbs. What I had in mind was a bed-sitting-room in Bottleton East, where I could study the martyred proletariat and soak in squalor at every pore."

Freddie yelped like a stepped-on puppy.

"Bottleton East? You're off your onion— I mean, you have an entirely erroneous conception of what Bottleton East is like. It's the cheeriest place in England. I sang at a song contest there once, so I know. The audience was the most rollicking set of blighters you ever saw. Never stopped throwing vegetables. No, Valley Fields is the spot for you."

"Really gray, is it, this outpost of eternity?"

"Couldn't be grayer."

"Squalor?"

"It wrote the words and music."

"Gissing!" exclaimed Miss Yorke, snapping her fingers.

Freddie shook his head.

"There's very little kissing done in Valley Fields. The aborigines are much too busy being gray."

"I didn't say kissing. I said Gissing—George Gissing. He wrote about the suburbs, and it's just the George Gissing sort of book I'm aiming at."

"Well, there you are. Didn't I tell you? You can't miss if you string along with George Gissing. Ask anybody."

"He was as gray as a stevedore's undervest."

"Very stark, I've always said so."

"Widgeon, I think you've got something."

"Me, too."

"The telephone's in the hall. Ring up that rat-catching friend of yours, the house agent fellow, and book me in at this Castlewood hovel, starting tomorrow. And—correct me if I'm wrong—I think this calls for another half bottle."

"Me also."

"Make a long arm," said Leila Yorke.

5.

In the whole of London there is no interior more richly dignified—*posh* is perhaps the word—than the lobby of Barribault's Hotel in Clarges Street, that haunt of Texas millionaires and visiting maharajahs. Its chairs and settees are the softest that money can provide, its lighting dim and discreet, its carpets of so thick a nap that midgets would get lost in them and have to be rescued by dogs. It is the general opinion of London's elite that until you have seen the lobby of Barribault's Hotel, you have not seen anything.

Some forty hours after Freddie Widgeon's visit to Loose Chippings, the quiet splendor of this beauty spot was enhanced by the presence of a superbly upholstered man of middle age who looked as if he might be an American senator or something of that sort. He had a frank, open face, fine candid eyes and a lofty brow rather resembling Shakespeare's. His name was Thomas G. Molloy, and he was waiting for his wife, who was due that morning to leave Holloway gaol, where she had been serving a short sentence for shoplifting.

He looked at his wrist watch, a little thing his mate had picked up at a Bond Street jeweler's while doing her Christmas shopping. The hands pointed to one-fifteen, and he began to feel worried, for, though he knew that she would be having a shampoo and a facial and possibly a perm after leaving her recent abode, he had expected her long before this. He was consulting the timepiece again some uneasy minutes later, when a voice behind him said "Hi, Soapy!" and he spun round. She was standing there, looking, it seemed to him, as if instead of in the deepest dungeon beneath Holloway gaol, she had been spending the last few weeks at some bracing seashore resort like Skegness.

Dolly Molloy unquestionably took the eye. She was a spectacular blonde of the type that is always getting murdered in its step-ins in mystery stories. Her hair was golden, her eyes hazel, her lips and cheeks aflame with color, and she carried herself with a challenging jauntiness. Wolf whistling is, of course, prohibited in the lobby of Barribault's Hotel, so none of those present attempted this form of homage, but quite a few of the visiting maharajahs looked as if they would have liked to, and it was plain that it was only by the exercise of the most iron self-restraint that the Texas millionaires were holding themselves in. You could see their lips puckering.

Soapy Molloy was devouring her with adoring eyes. Few

husbands more loving than he had ever cracked rocks in Sing Sing.

"Baby! I didn't see you come in."

"I was back there, hiding behind a pillar. There was a guy having a cocktail I didn't want to see me. Nobody you know. Fellow by the name of Prosser."

"Not the one they call Oofy?"

"I don't know what his first name is."

"Guy with pimples?"

"That's right. Why? Do you know him?"

"Must be the same. Young Widgeon next door to Castlewood introduced me to him. I've something to tell you about Prosser."

"Me, too, you, but it can wait. Let's eat, Soapy, I'm starving."

"I'll bet you are."

"They don't overfeed you in the coop."

"That's what I found last time I was up the river, and I guess it's the same over on this side. Too bad they got you, baby. What happened?"

"I didn't let my fingers flicker quick enough. And I didn't know the store dick was standing right behind me. Oh well, that's the way the cookie crumbles. You can't win 'em all."

"No, you can't win 'em all. That's what I told Chimp." Dolly started.

"Chimp?"

"I ran into him the other day."

"And told him about me?"

"He'd already heard. These things get around."

"What did he say?"

"He laughed."

"*Laughed?*"

"Laughed his head off."

Dolly bit her lip.

"He did, did he?" she said, and an ingrained dislike of their old associate Chimp Twist became accentuated. Circumstances had made it necessary for them to take this dubious character into partnership from time to time, but her relations with him had never been anything but strained, and it comforted her a good deal to remember that at their last meeting she had hit him on the head with the butt end of a pistol. She would willingly have done the same at this moment.

"The little potato bug!" she said, her fine eyes clouding as that unsympathetic laughter at her expense seemed to ring in her ears. "Is he still running that private-eye racket of his?"

The question surprised Mr. Molloy.

"Why, of course he is, sweetie. Why wouldn't he be? It's only a month since you've been away."

"Well, a month seems a long time for Chimp Twist to stay out of the coop. How's he doing?"

"He didn't say, but I guess he doesn't bother much about clients. The J. Sheringham Adair Private Investigation Agency's just a front."

Dolly laughed bitterly.

"J. Sheringham Adair! What a name to call himself."

"Had to call himself something."

"Well, why not Heels Incorporated or Double-crossers Limited or sump'n'? I tell you, Soapy, whenever I think of that undersized boll weevil, I go hot all over, clear down to the soles of my shoes."

"Oh, Chimp's not so bad."

"Not so bad as what?"

Mr. Molloy, though trying to be tolerant, found this question difficult to answer. He changed the subject.

"Swell place, this."

"Yeah."

"Makes one sort of sad, though."

"Why's that?"

"Well, seeing all these rich guys that nature intended I should sell 'em oil stock, and I can't because I don't know them. Sitting waiting for you and watching them come in through the swinging doors, I felt like a big-game hunter with a stream of giraffes, gnus and hippopotamuses passing by him and he can't do nothing because he came out without his gun."

"I know what you mean. It's tough."

"But no use worrying about it, I guess. Let's go eat."

"You can't make it too soon for me. But somewheres else, not here."

"Why, what's wrong with Barribault's? Best joint in London."

"So I've heard. But I don't like the company. Prosser's in there."

"I don't dig this Prosser stuff. What's he got on you?"

"Oh, this and that."

Soapy forbore to press his questioning. A solution of the mystery had occurred to him. It was, he knew, his consort's practice, when not collecting knickknacks at the department stores, to swoon in the arms of rich-looking strangers in the public streets and pick their pockets as they bent to offer her assistance, and no doubt Oofy Prosser had been one of the parties of the second part in some such business deal. This would, of course, account for a sensitive woman's reluctance to resume their acquaintance.

"Let's go to the Ivy," he said. "More onteem there, and I've lots to tell you, baby."

6.

It was not till they were settled at a corner table that Soapy touched on any subject other than his loneliness in his mate's absence and the ecstasy he felt in having her with him once more. The glass partition that separated them from the driver of their taxi was closed, but one never knew that a rich, rolling voice like his might not penetrate glass, and what he had to relate was not for the ears of taxi drivers.

"And now," he said, as the shrimps on his beloved one's plate vanished like nylon stockings from the counter of a department store, "lemme tell you what I've been doing since you went away."

"Not been idle?"

"Busy as that famous one-armed paper hanger."

"That's my boy! Shrimps," said Dolly, finishing the last one and regarding her empty plate hungrily, "are all right as a starter, but they don't have what you'd call authority."

"Just scratch the surface?"

"That's right. What's coming?"

"Sole mornay, and some sort of chicken after that."

"That's what I like to hear. You're doing me proud, honey."

"It's a celebration, and I can afford to. How would you feel about a month or so in the south of France?"

"As good as that, is it?"

"Just as good as that. I've cleaned up."

"Tell me."

Soapy Molloy's substantial form seemed to expand. He knew he was going to be impressive.

"Well, to start with, I unloaded a thousand pounds' worth of Silver River on young Widgeon at Peacehaven."

"You didn't!"

"That's what I did."

"I wouldn't have thought he had a thousand pounds."

"He hasn't now."

"Well, that's swell. I don't wonder you're feeling pleased with yourself. A thousand's nice sugar."

"Ah, but wait. You ain't heard nothing yet. I then took another thousand off his uncle, guy by the name of Blicester."

"You're kidding!"

"And," said Soapy, delivering the punch line, "two thousand off your friend Prosser."

Dolly choked on her sole mornay, as any loving wife would have done in similar circumstances. Her look of admiration warmed his heart.

"Soapy, you're a marvel!"

"I'm not so bad. What I always say is Give me a nice smooth-working sucker and plenty of room to swing my arms around, and I could sell the Brooklyn Bridge."

"Why, we're rich!"

"Rich enough to have a vacation in the south of France. Or would you prefer Le Touquet? Just the right time for Le Touquet now, and I haven't been there in three years. I did well when I was there last. That was before we were married. There was a woman I met at the Casino I sold quite a block of Silver River to."

"I'm not surprised. You're so fascinating, my great big wonderful man!"

"Just so long as I fascinate you, baby," said Mr. Molloy. "That's all I ask."

The meal proceeded on its delightful course. Coffee arrived. Soapy lit a large cigar, and it was only after he had sat smoking it for some little time that it was borne in upon him that his wife, usually an energetic talker, had fallen into a thoughtful silence. He looked across the table, somewhat concerned.

"What's the matter, baby?"

"Matter?"

"You're kind of quiet."

"I was thinking."

"What about?"

She seemed to brood for a moment, as if debating within herself whether silence would not be best. Then she made up her mind to speak.

"Soapy, there's something I want to tell you."

"I'm listening."

"I hadn't meant to tell you till your birthday."

"What is it?"

"It's something you'll like. You'll turn handsprings."

Soapy stared, not precisely aghast but definitely uneasy.

He had never been a great reader, but he liked occasionally to dip into the cheaper type of novelette, and in all the novelettes he had come across words like these on wifely lips could mean only one thing.

In a low, quivering voice, quite unlike his customary fruity utterance, he said, "Tiny garments?"

"Huh?"

He choked on his cigar.

"You heard. Are you knitting tiny garments?"

"You mean—?"

"That's what I mean."

Dolly broke into a peal of happy laughter.

"For Pete's sake! Of course I'm not."

"You aren't . . . ? We aren't . . . ?"

"Going to have little feet pattering about the home? Not a patter."

Soapy breathed deeply. He was not a philoprogenitive man, and a considerable weight had been lifted from his mind.

"Gosh, you had me scared for a minute!" he said, dabbing a handkerchief on his fine forehead.

Dolly was now all sparkle.

"No, nothing of that kind. Not but what later on . . ."

"Yes, later on," agreed Soapy. "A good deal later on. Then what's on your mind?"

"I don't know but what I still ought to save it up for your birthday, but— Oh, well, here it comes. Soapy, do you remember when I told you a couple of months ago I was going to spend a week or two visiting friends in the country?"

"Sure."

"Well, I didn't spend any week or two visiting friends in the country. Do you know what I actually done?"

"What?"

"I got a job as maid to a dame. Name of Prosser."

Soapy leaped in his chair, and sat staring. Enlighten-ment had come to him like a levin flash. In addition to dipping into novelettes, he read the daily papers regularly, and the front-page story of Mrs. Prosser's bereavement had not escaped his eye. Beads of excitement stood out on his Shakespearean brow, and he upset a coffee cup in his emotion.

"Baby! You aren't telling me— You don't mean— You didn't . . .?"

"Yup, that's what I did. I got away with her ice."

There was nothing small about Soapy Molloy. He ex-perienced no trace of chagrin at the thought that the triumphs of which he had been boasting so proudly a short while before had been demoted to the chicken-feed class by his wife's stupendous feat. Wholehearted admiration was all he felt. He gazed at her worshipingly, wondering what he could ever have done to deserve such a helpmeet.

"All those jools?" he gasped.

"Every last one."

"They must be worth the earth."

"They're not hay. Well, now you're hep to why I didn't want to meet Prosser."

"But why didn't you say anything about it before?"

"I told you. I was saving it up for your birthday."

Mr. Molloy breathed devoutly.

"Baby, there's no one like you."

"I thought you'd be pleased."

"I feel like dancing a skirt dance. Where are they?"

"Oh, they're tucked away somewhere quite safe." Dolly looked about her. "Everyone seems to have gone. We'd better be moving before they throw us out."

"What do you feel like doing now?"

"I thought I might look in at Selfridge's."

"I wouldn't, baby."

"I need some new stockings awful bad."

"But not this afternoon. Look, what I suggest is we go to Barribault's and—well, sort of loll around. We'll think of something to do."

"Where? In the lobby?"

"In my suite."

"In your *what?*"

"I've taken a suite there. You'll like it. It's got— What's the matter, baby? Why are you looking like that?"

He spoke anxiously, for into his wife's face there had come a look of horror and dismay, suggesting to him for a moment that the shrimps, the sole, the chicken, and the French pastry which had followed them had been too much for an interior enfeebled by prison fare. But this diagnosis was erroneous. It was not Dolly's internal mechanism that was troubling her.

"Soapy! You're not telling me you've left Castlewood?"

"Sure. I'm not saying the way I've cleaned up is anything like the way you've cleaned up, but I have cleaned up pretty good, and when you've cleaned up pretty good, you don't want to be horsing around down in the suburbs. You feel like splurging."

"Oh, my Gawd!"

"Why, what is it, sweetie?"

Dolly's face had a twisted look, as if she had swallowed something acid.

"I'll tell you what it is," she said, seeming to experience some difficulty in articulating. "The Prosser ice is at Castlewood."

"What!"

"On top of the wardrobe in our bedroom, that's what."

Soapy could understand now why his baby was looking

like that, as he had expressed it. He was looking like that himself.

"On top of the wardrobe?" he gurgled weakly.

"Seemed to me the safest place to put it. Yessir, there it is, and not a chance of getting at it, because by this time somebody'll have moved in."

"Not already."

"I shouldn't wonder. That fellow Cornelius, the guy with the full set of white whiskers, was telling me that houses like Castlewood never stay vacant for more than a day or two. Say, listen, go call him up."

"Cornelius?"

"Yeah. Ask him what the score is."

Mr. Molloy rose as if a bradawl had pierced the seat of his chair. He hurried out.

"You're right," he said lugubriously, returning some minutes later. "The joint's been rented."

"I thought as much."

"To Leila Yorke, the novelist. She clocked in this morning," said Soapy, and, beckoning a waiter, ordered double brandies for two. They both felt they needed them.

It was some time before either of them spoke. Then Dolly emerged from the fog of silent gloom which had been enveloping her. Women are more resilient than men.

"You'll have to go down there and see this dame and make a spiel."

"How do you mean, baby?"

"Why, tell her some story that'll make her let us have the house back."

"You think she would?"

"She might, if you're as good as you always were. Everyone says there's no one can pull a line of talk the way you can."

Mr. Molloy, though still far from being his usual hearty

self, became a little more cheerful. On the horizon of his mind there was shining a tiny spark of hope, like a lighted match seen at the end of a tunnel. Pulling a line of talk was a thing he knew himself to be good at.

"Worth trying," he agreed.

"Sure it is. We're not licked. Because don't forget that this dame writes books, and there never was an author yet who had enough sense to cross the street with. All these novelists are halfway around the bend."

Mr. Molloy nodded. There was, he knew, much in what she said.

7.

Leila Yorke was breakfasting in bed. Sally had boiled the
eggs and toasted the toast and taken them up to her, still
a good deal dazed by the swiftness with which she had
been uprooted and transferred from the old home to this
new environment. On Friday her employer had told her to
pack, on Saturday they had driven off in the car with the
Claines Hall butler staring after them like a butler who
is at a loss to understand, and here it was only Sunday
morning and they had been established at Castlewood
some twenty-four hours. Leila Yorke was a woman who
believed in doing it now, and though Sally was extremely
fond of her, there were moments when she found herself
wishing that she would less often model her behavior on

that of those American hurricanes which become so impulsive on arriving at Cape Hatteras.

As she sat trying to relax, the front doorbell rang. She went to answer it and found on the step a venerable figure almost completely concealed behind a long white beard. He was carrying a large suitcase and a bundle of papers, and she wondered for a moment if he had come to stay.

"Good morning," said this bearded pard.

"Good morning," said Sally.

"My name is Cornelius. Can I see Miss Yorke?"

"She's in bed."

"Not ill?" said Mr. Cornelius, blenching.

"Oh, no, just having breakfast."

"And thinking lovely thoughts," said Mr. Cornelius, reassured. "Does she keep a pad and pencil by her bedside?"

"Not that I know of."

"She should. The lightest of her meditations ought to be preserved. I have thirty-two of her books here," said Mr. Cornelius, indicating the suitcase. "I was hoping that she would autograph them."

"I'm sure she will. If you will leave them—"

"Thank you, Miss . . ."

"Foster. I'm Miss Yorke's secretary."

"What a privilege!"

"Yes."

"She must be a delightful woman."

"Yes, very."

"Her books have always been an inspiration to me, and not only to me but to the little literary society we have here which meets every second Thursday. I was wondering if Miss Yorke could be persuaded to come and talk to us this week."

"I'm terribly sorry, but I don't think she would be able

to manage it. She's just planning out a new novel, and of course that takes up all her time."

"I quite understand. Then I will just leave the Sunday papers for her. I thought she might care to see them."

"How awfully kind of you, Mr. Cornelius. I know she'll want the Sunday papers."

"They are rather difficult to obtain in Valley Fields. They are not delivered, and one has to go to a tobacconist's near the station. I always get Mr. Widgeon's for him. He lives at Peacehaven next door, and one likes to be neighborly. Goodbye, Miss Foster," said Mr. Cornelius, and with a courtly waggle of his beard he melted away.

His parting words made Sally jump. For an instant she thought she had heard him say "Mr. Widgeon." Then she knew that she must have been mistaken. Coincidences are all very well—in her novels Leila Yorke went in for them rather largely—but there is a limit. It was absurd to suppose that by pure accident she had come to live next door to the man she had resolved never to see again. A simple explanation suggested itself. Owing to his obiter dicta having to be filtered through a zareba of white hair, it was not always easy to catch exactly what Mr. Cornelius said. No doubt the name had been Williams or Wilson or possibly Wigham. It was with restored equanimity that she started to go and see how Miss Yorke was getting on with her breakfast and met her coming down the stairs in a pink dressing gown.

There was a frown on Leila Yorke's brow, as if she had temporarily suspended the thinking of lovely thoughts and had turned to others of an inferior grade.

"You look peeved," said Sally, noting this.

"I'm feeling peeved," said Miss Yorke. "What was that bell I heard?"

"That was the County starting to call. A Mr. Cornelius. I don't know who he is."

"He's the house agent. Keeps rabbits."

"Oh, does he? Well, he likes to be neighborly, so he brought you the Sunday papers."

"Bless him. Just what I wanted."

"And thirty-two of your books, to be autographed."

"Curse him. May his rabbits get myx-whatever-it-is."

"And he wants you to give a little talk to his literary society which meets every second Thursday."

"Oh, hell!"

"Keep calm. I got you out of it. I told him you were thinking out a new novel."

Leila Yorke snorted bitterly.

"You did, did you? Then you wantonly deceived the poor man. How can I think out a George Gissing novel, in surroundings like these? I always thought the suburbs were miles and miles of ghastly little semi-detached houses full of worn-out women ironing shirts and haggard men with coughs wondering where the rent was coming from, and look at this joint we've fetched up in. A palace, no less."

"Would you say that?"

"Well, it's got a summerhouse and two birdbaths and an aspidistra in the drawing room, not to mention a repro-duction of Millais's 'Huguenot' and a china mug with 'A Present from Bognor Regis' on it in pink sea shells, which I'll bet they haven't got at Windsor Castle. I ought to have known it. That young hound was pulling my leg."

"What young hound?"

"You know him. Widgeon. You brought him along to see me, and we got along like a couple of sailors on shore leave. We split a bottle of Bollinger and got kidding back and forth about his Uncle Rodney and Johnny Shoesmith and what have you, and in a weak moment I confided in him about this novel of squalor I'm trying to write, and he told me that if I wanted a place where I could absorb squalor by the gallon, I ought to come to Valley Fields. He said if I played my cards right, I could get this Castlewood house, and like a chump I told him to phone Cornelius and fix it up. And here I am, stuck in a luxury suburb about as inspirational as Las Vegas. For all the gray atmosphere I'm likely to find here, I might just as well have stayed where I was. Shows how unsafe it is ever to trust anybody in a solicitor's office. Twisters, all of them."

Twice during these remarks, as the perfidy of Frederick Widgeon was made clearer and clearer to her, Sally had gasped—the first time like a Pekingese choking on a bone of a size more suitable to a bloodhound, the second time like another Pekingese choking on another bone of similar dimensions. She was stunned by this revelation of the Machiavellian depths to which the male sex can descend when it puts its mind to it, and Leila Yorke looked at her oddly, puzzled by the expression on her face.

"Why," she asked, "have you turned vermilion?"

"I haven't."

"Pardon me. You look like a startled beetroot. This means something. Good Lord!" said Leila Yorke, inspired. "I see it all. Widgeon loves you, and he talked me into taking this blasted house so that he could be next door to you and in a position to tickle you across the fence. Shows character and enterprise, that. I see a bright future for the boy, if only I don't murder him with a blunt instrument for letting me in for this Valley Fields jaunt. I may or may not. I haven't decided. Yes, we have established that important point, I think. Love has wound its silken fetters about Widgeon."

If Sally had been a character in one of Leila Yorke's books, she would have ground her teeth. Not knowing how to, she sniffed.

"It would be odd if it hadn't," she said bitterly. "He loves every girl he meets."

"Is that so?" said Leila Yorke, interested. "I knew a man once who had the same tendency. He was a chartered accountant, and all chartered accountants have hearts as big as hotels. You think they're engrossed in auditing the half-yearly balance sheet of Miggs, Montagu and Murgatroyd, general importers, and all the time they're writing notes to blondes saying, 'Tomorrow, one-thirty, same place.' I wouldn't let that worry you. It doesn't amount to anything. Men are like that."

"I don't want a man like that."

"You want Widgeon, whatever he's like. I've been watching you with a motherly eye for some time, and I've noted all the symptoms—the faraway, stuffed-frog look, the dreamy manner, the quick jump like a rising trout when spoken to suddenly. My good child, you're crazy about him, and if you've any sense, you'll tell him so and sign him up. I'm a lot older than you, and I'll give a piece of advice. If you love a man, never be such an ass as to let him go. I'm telling you this as one who knows, because that's what I did, and I've never stopped regretting it. Were you engaged?"

"Yes."

"Broke it off?"

"Yes."

"I was married. Much worse, because it hurts more that way. You've so much more to remember. But a broken engagement's nothing. You can stick it together again in a couple of minutes, and if you'll take my advice, you'll attend to it right away. You'll probably find him in his garden, rolling the lawn or whatever they do in these parts on a Sunday morning. Pick up your feet, kid, and go and tell him what you really think of him."

"I will," said Sally, and set forth with that resolve firmly fixed in her mind. She was breathing flame softly through the nostrils.

8.

Freddie was not rolling the lawn when she came out into the garden; he was seated in the shade of the one tree that Peacehaven possessed, reading the Sunday paper which Mr. Cornelius had so kindly brought him, and Sally, reaching the fence, paused. The problem of how to attract his attention had presented itself. "Hi!" seemed lacking in dignity. "Hoy!" had the same defect. And "Freddie!" was much too friendly. What she would really have liked, of course, would have been to throw a brick at him, but the grounds of Castlewood, though parklike, were unfortunately lacking in bricks. She compromised by saying "Good morning," in a voice that lowered the balmy temperature of the summer day by several degrees Fahrenheit, and he looked up with a start and having looked up sat for an instant spellbound, the picture of a young man in flannels and an Eton Ramblers blazer who is momentarily unable to believe his eyes. Then, rising acrobatically, he hurried to the fence.

"Sally!" he gasped. "Is it really you?"

"Yes," said Sally, and once more the temperature dropped noticeably. A snail that was passing at the time huddled back into its shell with the feeling that there was quite a nip in the air these mornings and would have slapped its ribs, if it had had any.

"But this is the most extraordinary thing that ever happened," said Freddie. "It takes the breath away. What are those things they have in deserts? I don't mean Foreign Legions. Mirages, that's the word. When I looked up and saw you standing there, I thought it was a mirage."

"Oh?"

"Well, I mean, you can't say it isn't remarkable that I should look up and see you standing there. It—how shall I put it—it took the breath away."

"Oh?"

There is something about the monosyllable "Oh?" when uttered in a cold, level voice by the girl he loves that makes the most intrepid man uneasy. Freddie had been gifted by nature with much of the gall of an army mule, but even he lost a little of his animation. However, he persevered.

"Don't tell me you've come to live at Castlewood?"

It was practically impossible for Sally to look colder and prouder than she had been doing since the start of this interview, but she did her best.

"Do you need to be told?"

"Eh?"

"I've heard the whole story from Miss Yorke."

Freddie gulped. This, an inner voice was whispering, was not so good.

"The whole story?"

"Yes."

"She spilled the beans?"

"She did."

"You know all?"

"I do."

"Then in that case," said Freddie, suddenly, brightening as a man will when he has found a good talking point, "perhaps you'll get it into your nut how much I love you. I will conceal nothing from you."

"You won't have the chance."

"I did lure the Yorke here, and I'd do it again. I'd lure a thousand Yorkes here. It was imperative to have you within easy talking distance so that I could plead my cause and get you to stop being a little fathead."

"I am not a fathead."

"Pardon me. You appear to be under the impression that my love isn't sincere and wholehearted and all that sort of thing. Therefore you stand revealed as a fathead."

"And you stand revealed as a cross between a flitting butterfly and a Mormon elder," said Sally with spirit. "You and Brigham Young, a pair."

This silenced Freddie for a moment, but he continued to persevere.

"I beg your pardon?"

"You make love to every girl you meet."

"It's a lie."

"It is not a lie."

"It is a lie, and actionable, too, I shouldn't wonder. I must ask Shoesmith. Really, to come here flinging around these wild and unwarrantable accusations—"

"Unwarrantable, did you say?"

"That was the word I used."

"Oh? Well, how about Drusilla Wix?"

"Eh?"

"And Dahlia Prenderby and Mavis Peasemarch and Vanessa Vokes and Helen Christopher and Dora Pinfold and Hildegarde Watt-Watson?"

This rain of names plainly shook Freddie. He seemed to shrink within his Eton Ramblers blazer in much the same way as the recent snail had shrunk within its shell, and like the snail, he had the momentary illusion that Valley Fields was in the grip of a cold wave.

In a voice that gave the impression that he had tried to swallow something large and sharp, which had lodged in his windpipe, he said, "Oh, those?"

"Yes, those."

"Who told you about them?"

"Mr. Prosser."

"Oofy?"

"I told you he came to see Miss Yorke one day. I showed him round the place and we got talking and your name came up and he said you were always in love with every girl you met and proved it by supplying details. Those were the only names he mentioned, but I have no doubt he could have added hundreds more."

Freddie was stunned. He stammered as he spoke. He had seldom been so shocked.

"Oofy! A fellow I've practically nursed in my bosom! If that's his idea of being a staunch pal, then all I can say is that it isn't mine."

"He was merely passing on information which is generally known to all the young thugs of your acquaintance. It is common knowledge that if all the girls you've loved were placed end to end, they would reach from Piccadilly Circus to Hyde Park Corner."

It seemed to Freddie that Castlewood, a solidly built house, though of course, as in the case of most suburban houses, it was unsafe to treat it roughly by leaning against the walls or anything like that, was doing an Ouled Naïls stomach dance. With a strong effort he mastered an inclination to swoon where he stood. He found speech and movement, and not even Mr. Molloy, when selling oil stock, could have waved his arms more vigorously.

"But, dash it, don't you understand that those were just boyish fancies? You're different."

"Oh?" said Sally, and if ever an "Oh?" nearly came out as "Ho!" this one did.

Freddie continued to act like an emotional octopus. The speed at which his arms were gyrating almost deceived the eye.

"Yes, of course you're different. You're the real thing. You're what I've been hunting around for ever since I went to my first kindergarten. And all those girls you've mentioned had popped in and out of my life long before I met you. Oh, Sally darling, do get it into your loaf that you're the only damned thing in this damned world that matters a damn to me."

In spite of herself Sally found herself wavering. She had planned to be firm and sensible, but it is not easy for a girl to remain firm and sensible when such melting words are proceeding from the lips of the only man she has ever really loved. And a disturbing, weakening thought had floated into her mind—to wit, that she herself had not the unimpeachable record which she was demanding from this opposite number of hers. She had never revealed the fact to him, for a girl likes to have her little secrets, but she, too, had had her experiences. There had been quite a troupe of Bills and Toms and Jimmys in her life before Frederick Widgeon had come into it, and what did they amount to now? They had gone with the wind, they meant nothing to her, she did not even send them Christmas cards. Could it be that the Misses Wix, Prenderby, Pease-march, Vokes, Christopher, Pinfold and Watt-Watson ranked equally low in the estimation of Freddie Widgeon?

As she stood debating this point, a voice spoke from behind her. "Hullo there, Widgeon."

"Oh, hullo, Miss Yorke. Welcome to Valley Fields."

"Welcome to Valley Fields, my foot. I'd like a word with you some time about Valley Fields and its gray squalor."

"Any time that suits you."

"That was a nice trick you played on me, was it not? Still, we can go into that later. For your information, I'm inclined to take a lenient view."

"Good show."

"Now that I learn that it was love that drove you on. Love conquers all."

"You betcher."

"If you're in love, you're in love."

"You never spoke a truer word."

"Well," said Leila Yorke, who was always direct in her methods and seldom beat about bushes, "how's it coming? Have you kissed her?"

"Not yet."

"For heaven's sake! Are you man or mouse?"

"Well, you see, there's a snag. I'm not so dashed sure she wants me to. The thing's what Shoesmith would call sub judice."

"Of course she wants you to."

"You really feel that?"

"It's official."

Freddie drew a deep breath.

"How's chances, Sally?"

"Pretty good, Freddie."

"That's better. That's more the stuff. That's the sort of thing I like to hear," said Leila Yorke, and wandered off, thinking what Mr. Cornelius would have called lovely thoughts. The situation reminded her a little of the getting-together of Claude Hallward and Cynthia Roseleigh in her *Cupid, the Archer*.

"Woof!" said Freddie some moments later.

"Oh, Freddie!" said Sally. "I've been so miserable, Freddie."

"Me, too. Plunged in gloom."

"Do you really love me?"

"Like billy-o."

"You'll always love me?"

"Till the sands of the desert grow cold."

"Well, mind you do. When I'm married, I want my husband to stay put, not go flitting from flower to flower."

"That shall be attended to."

"I don't want you ever to speak to another girl."

"I won't."

"And don't—"

"I know what you're going to say. You would prefer that I didn't kiss them. Right ho. Never again. It's just a mannerism."

"Correct it."

"I will. I'll be like Johnny Shoesmith. He wouldn't kiss Helen of Troy if you brought her to him asleep on a chair with a sprig of mistletoe suspended over her. And now hop across that fence, and I'll show you round Peacehaven."

Leila Yorke, meanwhile, after doing the setting-up exercises with which she always began the day, had gone back to her bedroom to dress. She had just completed her toilet when the front doorbell rang. With a brief "Oh, hell!"— for this, she supposed, would be Mr. Cornelius playing a return date with another suitcaseful of books to be auto-graphed—she went to answer it.

It was not Mr. Cornelius. It was a snappily dressed man of middle age with a frank, open face, and a lofty brow resembling Shakespeare's, who gazed at her with fine, candid eyes as if the sight of her had just made his day.

"Miss Leila Yorke?"

"Yes."

"Good morning, Miss Yorke. This is a wonderful moment for me. I am one of your greatest admirers. That must be my excuse for this unceremonious call. Could I speak to you for a few minutes, if I am not interrupting your work? It would be a great privilege."

9.

Sunday, with the marts of trade closed and no chance of going out and doing a little shopping, was always a dullish day for Dolly Molloy, and after the departure of Soapy for Castlewood she had found the time passing slowly. She did her nails, tried her hair a different way, changed her stockings three times and experimented with a new lipstick, formerly the property of a leading department store, but she was unable altogether to dispel ennui, and it was with relief that as the hour approached when one would be thinking about a bite of lunch she heard a key turning in the door.

"I thought you were never coming, honey," she cried happily, bounding up to greet the warrior back from the front.

But her happiness was short-lived. One glance as he came into the room was enough to tell her that here was not a man bringing the good news from Aix to Ghent but one who had a tale of failure to relate. There was a cloud on Soapy's brow, and his eyes were somber. His whole appearance conveyed the suggestion that in the not distant past he had undergone some spiritual experience which he had found disturbing. Only too plainly he was in the grip of that grief—void, dark and drear, which finds no natural outlet, no relief, in word or sigh or tear—which in the early eighteen hundreds had depressed the poet Coleridge.

He sank into a chair and wiped his forehead with a silk handkerchief which his helpmeet had picked up at Harrod's one afternoon last fall and given him for Christmas.

"Gosh!" he said in a voice that might well have come from a tomb.

Dolly was a good wife. Though quivering with curiosity and burning to ask questions, she knew that first things must come first. Some quarter of an hour ago Room Service had deposited on a side table a tray containing ice and glasses, and she hurried to a cupboard and extracted from it gin, vermouth and a shaker. A musical tinkling broke the silence that had fallen on the room, and presently Soapy, after he had had one quick and had got started on another rather slower, gave evidence of being sufficiently restored to be able to render his report.

Dolly, observing these improved conditions, felt that the need for restraint was past and that questions were now in order.

"What happened, Soapy? Did you go there? Did you see her? What's she like?"

Soapy winced. The question had touched an exposed nerve. As had been the case with Freddie Widgeon, he had expected to find in Leila Yorke a frail little wisp of a thing who would be corn before his sickle, and right from the start her personality had intimidated him. He had found those bright, piercing blue eyes of hers particularly disturbing, and later, when she had produced that shotgun . . . He shivered at the recollection. He was a man not easy to disconcert—if you make your living selling stock in derelict oil wells, you learn to present a confident, even a brassy, face to the world—but Leila Yorke had done it.

"She's a tough egg," he said, drying his forehead again. "You remember Soup Slattery?"

"Of course." That eminent safeblower had been one of their intimate circle in the old Chicago days. "But what's Soup got to do with it?"

"She's a little like him. Better-looking, of course, but that same way of giving you the cold, glassy eye that Soup has when you're playing poker with him and he's got the idea that it's not all according to Hoyle. Those eyes of hers sort of go through you and come out the other side. The moment I saw her, I knew it wasn't going to be easy, but I never dreamed things were going to turn out the way they did. No sir, it never occurred to me."

Nothing is more irritating to a woman of impatient habit, wanting to get the news headlines quickly, than to try to obtain them from a man who seems intent on speaking in riddles, and a less affectionate wife than Dolly might well at this point have endeavored to accelerate her husband by striking him with the cocktail shaker. It is to her credit that she confined herself to words.

"What way? How do you mean? What *happened?*"

Soapy marshaled his thoughts. He had finished that second martini now and was feeling calmer. The knowledge that seven miles separated him from Leila Yorke had done much to restore his composure. And he was reminding himself, as Dolly had reminded him yesterday, that you can't win 'em all. It was a comforting reflection. He was not entirely his old hearty self as he began his story, but he had shaken off that dizzy feeling which comes to the man who pays a social call and suddenly finds his hostess jabbing a shotgun into his diaphragm.

"Well, sir, I got to Castlewood and rang the bell. The front doorbell. I rang it. Yes sir, I rang the front doorbell."

Though accustomed to her loved one's always deliberate methods as a raconteur, Dolly could not repress a sharp yelp of exasperation. She needed her lunch, and it looked as though this was going to take some time.

"Get on, get on! I didn't think you blew a bugle."

This puzzled Soapy. Except when he was selling oil stock, his mind always moved rather slowly.

"Bugle?"

"Get on."

"Why would I blow a bugle?"

"Skip it. Let it go."

"I didn't have a bugle. Where would I get a bugle?"

"I said skip it. Do concentrate, honey. We left our hero ringing at the door. What happened then?"

"She opened it."

"*She* did?"

"Yes."

"Hasn't she a maid?"

"Didn't seem to have."

"No help at all?"

"Not that I could see. Why?"

"Oh, nothing. I was just thinking."

The thought that had floated into Dolly's mind was that if the garrison of Castlewood was so sparsely manned, it might be possible to drop in one evening with a sandbag and do something constructive. She had always been a woman who liked the direct approach. But Soapy's next words showed this to be but an idle dream.

"All she's got is a secretary and a shotgun."

"A *shotgun?*"

"That's right. One of those sporting guns it looked like."

Dolly did not often touch her hair when she had done it to her liking, but she clasped it now with both hands. She was finding her mate's story difficult to follow. The shotgun motif perplexed her particularly.

"Tell me the whole thing right from the beginning," she said, reckless of the fact that this might involve another description of how he rang the doorbell.

Soapy asked if there was a dividend. There was, and he drank it gratefully. Then, as if inspired, he plunged into his narrative without more delay.

"Well, like I say, she opened the door, and there we were. 'Miss Leila Yorke?' I said. 'That's me, brother,' she said. 'You'll forgive me for butting in like this, Miss Yorke,' I said, 'but I am one of your greatest admirers. Can I talk to you for a moment?' I said, and then I went into my spiel. It was a swell spiel. If I say it myself, I was good."

"I'll bet you were."

"The line I took was that I was one of these rugged millionaires who'd made my money in oil, and I sketched out for her the sort of conditions you live in when you're starting out after oil—the barren scenery, the wooden shacks, the companionship of rough and uneducated men, the absence of anything that gives a shot in the arm to a guy's cultural side. I gave all that a big build-up."

"I can just hear you."

" 'For years,' I said, 'I went along like that, starved for intellectual sustenance, and it was getting so that my soul was withering like a faded leaf in the fall, when one day I happened on a tattered copy of one of your books.' "

"Did she ask you which one?"

"Sure she did. Having looked her up in *Who's Who,* I was able to tell her. It was one of the early ones. I said it kind of seemed to open a whole new world to me, and as soon as I was able to raise the money from my meager earnings I bought the whole lot and read them over and over, each time learning something new from them. I said I owed her more than I could ever repay."

"That must have tickled her."

"You'd have thought so, but it was just then that I noticed she was looking at me in that odd, Soup Slattery kind of way, sort of narrowing her eyes as if there was something about my face she didn't like."

"If she didn't like your face, she must be cuckoo. It's a swell face."

"Well, I've always got by with it, but that was the way she was looking. 'So you feel you owe me a lot, do you?' she said, and I said 'I do indeed,' and she said, 'That's just how I feel.' "

"Kind of conceited," said Dolly disapprovingly.

"That's how it struck me. These authors, I said to myself. Still, I didn't hold it against her, because I knew they were all that way. I went into my sales talk. I said money was no object to me, and I wanted to buy this house of hers, no matter what it cost, and keep it as a sort of shrine. I wasn't sure, I said, if I wouldn't have it taken down and shipped over to America and set up on my big estate in Virginia. Like William Randolph Hearst used to do."

"But Castlewood doesn't belong to her. She's only renting it, same as we did."

"Yes, I knew that, of course, but I was just leading up to the big moment. She told me the place belonged to Keggs and he was in Singapore or somewhere on his round-the-world cruise, and I said Well, that was too bad, because I'd set my heart on getting it and this was going to be a great disappointment to my friends on the other side, who were all great admirers of hers, same as me. 'But you won't mind me just rambling about and taking a look at this shrine where you live and work?' I said, and was starting to head for the bedroom when she said, 'Excuse me.' "

"Went to powder her nose?"

"No, she went to get this shotgun of hers. She came back with it, and pointed it at my wishbone. 'Listen, rat!' she said. 'Your kind attention for a moment, please. You have just three seconds to get out of here.' "

"For Pete's sake! Why?"

"The very question I asked her. And she said, 'So you made your money out of oil, did you? I'll say you did, my rugged millionaire, and a thousand pounds of it was donated by me. Le Touquet three years ago—remember?' Baby, she was the dame in the Casino I told you about, the one I sold that Silver River to. Naturally I hadn't placed her. When we did our deal, she was wearing dark glasses, and one meets so many people. But she remembered me all right. 'I shall count three,' she said, 'and if by the time I say -ee you aren't halfway back to America, you'll get a charge of shot in the seat of the pants.' Well, I can take a hint. I didn't stand loitering about. I left. So there you are, honey. Ninety-nine times out of a hundred that line of talk of mine would have dragged home the gravy, but this was the one time it didn't. Too bad, but nobody's to blame."

Dolly was all wifely sympathy.

"I'm not blaming you, sweetie. You did all that a man could do . . . unless . . . You couldn't have beaned her with a chair, I suppose?"

"Not a hope. If I'd made a move or so much as stirred a finger, I wouldn't be sitting down like this. I'd be lying on my face with you picking shot out of me with your eyebrow tweezers. She meant business," said Soapy, and he stirred uneasily in his chair as he thought of what might have been. He was a high-strung man, and vivid mental pictures came easily to him.

Dolly sat frowning thoughtfully. A lesser woman would have been crushed by this tale of disaster, but she never allowed a temporary setback to make her forget the lesson of the story of Bruce and the spider. Like the poet, she held it truth with him who sings to one clear harp in divers tones that men—or, in her case, women—can rise on steppingstones of their dead selves to higher things.

"We must have another try," she said, and Soapy started as if Leila Yorke and her shotgun had materialized themselves before him.

"You aren't suggesting I go to Castlewood again?"

"Not you, sweetie. Me."

"But what sort of spiel can you give her?"

"Ah, that wants thinking out. But I'll dig up something. The thought of all that ice laying there on top of that wardrobe, when at any moment someone might get the idea of dusting there and put their hooks on it, goes right against my better nature. Come on, honey, let's lunch. You need some nourishing food inside you after going through that— What's the word?"

"Ordeal," said Mr. Molloy, whose life work had given him a good vocabulary. "When you're up against a dame with glittering eyes and one finger on the trigger of a shotgun, that's an ordeal, and don't let anyone tell you different."

There is something about lunch at a place like Barribault's that raises the spirits and stimulates the brain. The hors d'oeuvres seem to whisper that the sun will some day shine once more, the cold salmon with tartare sauce points out that though the skies are dark the silver lining will be along at any moment, and with the fruit salad or whatever it may be that tops off the meal, there comes a growing conviction that the bluebird, though admittedly asleep at the switch of late, has not formally gone out of business. These optimistic reflections did not occur to Soapy, who remained downcast and moody throughout, but Dolly had scarcely taken two bites out of her pêche Melba when she uttered a glad cry.

"Soapy, I've got it!"

Mr. Molloy, who was toying with a strawberry ice, jerked a spoonful into space. It fell to earth, he knew not where.

"Got what, baby? Not an idea?"

"Yeah, and a darned good one."

The gloom which had been enveloping Soapy lightened a little. He had a solid respect for his wife's ingenuity.

"Look, honey, you told me there was no help at Castlewood. Well, look, this Yorke dame and the secretary have got to go out some time, haven't they? To do the shopping and all that."

"I guess so."

"So the place'll be empty. Well, what's to stop me going down there and hanging around till the coast's clear and slipping in? The Widgeon guy goes off to his office in the morning, so I can wait in the front garden of Peacehaven till I see them leave."

"Suppose they don't leave?"

"For heaven's sake, they've got to do it some time or other. As a matter of fact, I think the balloon'll go up tomorrow, because I read a thing in the paper about how Leila Yorke was due to speak at some luncheon or other, and I guess she'll take the secretary with her. Even if she doesn't, the secretary's sure to play hooky when she's not around. Ask me, the thing'll be handed to us on a plate. I'll go there tomorrow right after breakfast. Unless you'd rather?"

Mr. Molloy, shuddering strongly, said he would not rather.

"All right, then, me. I don't see how it can fail. The back door won't be locked. I can just slip in. Any questions?"

"Not a one. Baby," said Mr. Molloy devoutly, "I've said it before and I'll say it again. There's no one like you."

10.

The function at which Leila Yorke had committed herself to speak was the bimonthly lunch of the women's branch of the Pen and Ink Club, and she had completely forgotten the engagement till Sally reminded her of it. On learning that the curse had come upon her, she uttered one of those crisp expletives which were too sadly often on her lips and said that that was what you got for letting your guard down for a single moment with these darned organizing secretaries. Iron, unremitting firmness was what you needed if you were not to be a puppet in their hands.

"They're cunning. That's the trouble. They write to you in December asking you to do your stuff in the following June, and you, knowing that June will never arrive, say you will, and blister my internal organs if June doesn't come around after all."

"Suddenly it's spring."

"Exactly. And you wake up one fine morning and realize you're for it. You ever been to one of these fêtes that are worse than death, Sally?"

"No, I'm not a member of the Pen and Ink. Mine has been a very sheltered life."

"Avoid them," Leila Yorke advised, "especially the all-women ones. Yes, I know you're going to argue that it's better to be confronted with a gaggle of female writers in ghastly hats and pince-nez than a roomful of male writers with horn-rimmed glasses and sideburns, but I disagree with you. The female of the species is far deadlier than the male. What am I to say to these gargoyles?"

" 'Good afternoon, gargoyles'?"

"And then sit down? Not a bad idea. I don't think it's ever been done. Well, go and get the car out. I've some shopping to do, so we'll make an early start."

"We?"

"Oh, I'm not going to drag you into the lunch. One has one's human feelings. I want you to go and see Saxby and tell him of the change of plans about the new book. As my literary agent, I suppose he's entitled to be let in on the thing. Break it to him gently. Better take a flask of brandy with you in case he swoons."

"He'll be upset, all right."

"And so will my poor perishing publishers. I've a contract for six books with them, and if I have my strength, those books are going to get starker and starker right along, and the starker they become, the lower will those unhappy blighters' jaws drop. But what the hell? Art's art, isn't it? Suppose they do lose their shirts? Money isn't everything."

"You can't take it with you."

"Exactly. After seeing Saxby, look in on them and tell them that. It'll cheer them up. But do you know who's going to howl like a timber wolf about this?"

"The whole firm, I should say. They rely on you for their annual holiday-at-Blackpool expenses."

"Prosser, that's who. He's got a wad of money in the business, and when he finds I'm putting it in jeopardy, he'll hit the ceiling. Oh well, we can't help Prosser's troubles. Into each life some rain must fall. Go and get the car."

Sally got the car and, as they drove off and were passing Peacehaven, startled her employer by uttering a sudden exclamation.

"Now what?" said Leila Yorke.

"Nothing," said Sally.

But it had not been nothing. What had caused her to exclaim had been the sight of a spectacular blonde leaning on the Peacehaven front gate, as if, so it seemed to her jaundiced eye, the place belonged to her. The last thing a girl likes to see leaning in this manner on the gate of the man she loves, especially when she knows him to be one of the opposite sex's greatest admirers, is a blonde of that description. Even a brunette would have been enough to start a train of thought in Sally's mind, and she passed the remainder of the short journey to the metropolis in silence, a prey to disturbing reflections on the subject of leopards and spots and the well-known inability of the former to change the latter. It was only when the car had been housed at a garage near Berkeley Square and she and Leila Yorke had parted, the one to do her shopping, the other to go and ruin the morning of Mr. Saxby, the literary agent, and of the Messrs. Popgood and Grooly, Miss Yorke's poor perishing publishers, that there came to her a consoling recollection—to wit, that Freddie had told her that he shared Peacehaven with his cousin George, the sleepless guardian of the law. Policemen, she knew, have their softer side and like, when off duty, to sport with Amaryllis in the shade. No doubt the spectacular one was a friend of George's. As she entered the premises of the Saxby literary agency, Freddie having thus been dismissed without a stain on his character, she was feeling quite happy.

So, as she leaned on the gate of Peacehaven and watched the car disappear round the corner, was Dolly Molloy. Everything, as she envisaged it, was now hunky-dory. There remained only the task of walking a few yards, slipping in through a back door, mounting a flight of stairs, picking up a chamois leather bag and going home, a simple program which she was confident would be well within her scope. And she was opening the gate as a preliminary to the first stage of the venture, when from immediately behind her a voice spoke, causing her to skip like the high hills and swallow the chewing gum with which she had been refreshing herself.

"Oh, hullo," it said, and turning she perceived a tall, superbly muscled young man, at the sight of whom her hazel eyes, which had been shining with a glad light, registered dismay and horror. This was not because she disliked tall, superbly muscled young men or because the Oxford accent in which he had spoken jarred upon her transatlantic ear, it was due to the circumstance that the other was wearing the uniform and helmet of a policeman, and if there was one thing a checkered life had taught her to shrink from, it was the close proximity of members of the force. No good, in her experience, ever came of it.

"You waiting for Freddie Widgeon? I'm afraid he's gone up to London."

"Oh?" said Dolly. It was all she found herself able to say. The society of coppers, peelers, flatfeet, rozzers and what are known in the newest argot of her native land as "the fuzz" always affected her with an unpleasant breathlessness.

"He works in an office, poor devil, and has to leave pretty soon after the morning repast. Around six P.M. is the time to catch him. Is there anything I can do for you? I'm his cousin George."

"But—" Dolly's breath was slowly returning. The lack of menace in her companion's attitude had reassured her. Too many policemen in the past, notably in the Chicago days, had shown her their rather brusquer side, generally starting their remarks with the word Hey! and she found the easy polish of this one comforting. She was, of course, still in something of a twitter, for the conscience of a girl who has recently purloined several thousand pounds' worth of jewelry is always sensitive, but she had ceased to entertain the idea that her personal well-being was in danger.

"But you're a cop," she said.

"That's right. Somebody has to be, what?"

"I mean, you don't talk like one."

"Oh, that? Oh, well, Eton, you know. Oxford, you know. All that sort of rot, you know."

"I didn't know the bulls over here went to Oxford."

"Quite a few of them don't, I believe, but I did. And when I came down, it was a choice between going into an office or doing something else, so I became a flattie. Nice open-air life and quite a chance, they tell me, of rising to great heights at Scotland Yard, though they were probably pulling my leg. What I need to set my foot on the ladder of success is a good pinch, and how that is to be achieved in Valley Fields is more than I can tell you, for of all the unenterprising law-abiding blighters I ever saw the locals take the well-known biscuit. It discourages a chap. But I say, I'm awfully sorry to be gassing about myself like this. Must be boring you stiff. Did you want to see Freddie on some matter of import? Because, if so, you'll find him at Shoesmith, Shoesmith, Shoesmith and Shoesmith in Lincoln's Inn Fields, if you know where that is. They're a legal firm. Freddie works for them. At least," said Cousin George, appearing to share the doubts expressed on a previous occasion by Mr. Shoesmith, "he goes there and sits. Head for Fleet Street and ask a policeman. He'll direct you. Our police are wonderful."

"Oh, no, it's nothing important, thanks. I just wanted to say Hello."

"Then I'll be off, if you don't mind. We of the constabulary mustn't be late at the trysting place, or we get properly told off by our superiors. Pip-pip, then, for the nonce. Oh, there's just one other thing before I go. You wouldn't care to buy a couple of tickets for the annual concert of the Policemen's Orphanage, would you?"

"Who, me?"

"Sounds silly, I know, but the men up top issue bundles of the beastly things to us footsloggers, and we're supposed to unload them on the local residents."

"I'm not a local resident."

"They come, nicely graded, to suit all purses—the five-shilling, the half-crown, the two-shilling, the shilling and the sixpenny—only the last-named means standing up at the back. Anything doing?"

"Not a thing."

"Think well. You'll never forgive yourself if you miss hearing Sergeant Banks sing 'Asleep in the Deep,' or, for the matter of that, Constable Bodger doing imitations of footlight favorites who are familiar to you all. So, on re-flection shall we say a brace of the five-bobs?"

Dolly was firm. The thought of doing anything even remotely calculated to encourage the police went, as she would have said, against her better nature.

"Listen, brother," she said, her voice cold and her eyes stony. "If you are open to suggestions as to where you can stick those tickets of yours, I can offer one."

"No need. I take your point. Not in the market, what? Then I don't have to go into my patter. There's a regular recitation they teach us, designed to stimulate trade, all about supporting a charitable organization which is not only most deserving in itself but is connected with a body of men to whom you as a householder—not that you are, but if you were—will be the first to admit that you owe the safety of your person and the tranquillity of your home. The rozzers, in short. Still, if you're allergic to Policemen's Orphanages, there is nothing more for me to add but—"

" 'Pip-pip.' "

"I was about to say 'Toodle-oo.' "

"Toodle-oo, then. Nice to have met you. Keep your chin up and don't arrest any wooden nickels," said Dolly, and Cousin George went on his way, his manner a little pensive. He was thinking that Freddie, though unques-tionably a picker as far as looks were concerned, had some odd friends. Charming girl, of course, his late companion, and one of whom he would willingly have seen more, but definitely not the sort you brought home and introduced to mother.

As for Dolly, she remained where she was for some moments, still a little unstrung, as always after she had been talking to policemen. Then, having shaken off most of the ill effects of the recent encounter, she hurried down the road and received further evidence that this was not, as she had at one time supposed, her lucky day. In the Castlewood front garden there was a gate similar to that of Peacehaven. On this Mr. Cornelius was leaning with folded arms and the general appearance of one who planned to be there for some considerable time. Courteous as always to tenants, he greeted her with a friendly waggle of his white beard, seeming much more pleased to see her than she was to see him. Of Thomas G. Molloy, as we have seen, he disapproved, but he had always admired Dolly.

"Why, good morning, Mrs. Molloy. It is a long time since we met. Mr. Molloy told me that you had been away."

"Yup, visiting friends," said Dolly, though feeling that it was stretching the facts a little to apply this term to the authorities of Holloway gaol. "Quite a surprise it was to me when Soapy said he'd left Castlewood."

"To me, also, when he told me he was leaving."

"Well, that's how it goes. With all those big business interests of his, he found he had to be nearer the center of things, what I mean."

"I quite understand. Business must always come first."

"Kind of a wrench, of course, it was to him, having to move from Valley Fields."

"I am not surprised. I am sure it was. There is no place like it. When I think of Valley Fields, Mrs. Molloy, I am reminded of the words of Sir Walter Scott. I daresay you know them. They occur in his poem 'The Lay of the Last Minstrel,' where he says, 'Breathes there the man, with soul so dead, Who never to himself hath said, This is my own, my native land? Whose heart hath ne'er within him burned, As home his footsteps he hath turned, From wandering on a foreign strand?' " said Mr. Cornelius, thinking of the day trip he had once taken to Boulogne.

Reduced to the status of a captive audience, Dolly found her already pronounced impatience increasing. Mr. Cornelius had recited this well-known passage to her soon after her arrival in Valley Fields, and she knew that, unless he was nipped in the bud, there was a lot more of it to come.

"Yeah," she said. "No argument about that. But what I came about—"

" 'If such there breathe,' " proceeded the house agent smoothly, " 'go, mark him well; For him no minstrel raptures swell; High though his titles, proud his name, Boundless his wealth as wish can claim—Despite those titles, power and pelf—' "

"What I came about—"

" '—The wretch, concentred all in self, Living, shall forfeit fair renown, And, doubly dying, shall go down To the vile dust from whence he sprung—' "

"I just wanted—"

" '—Unwept, unhonored and unsung,' " concluded Mr. Cornelius severely, putting the anonymous outcast right in his place. "Those words, Mrs. Molloy, will appear on the title page of the history of Valley Fields which I am compiling."

"Yes, so you told me, a couple of months ago."

"It will be printed at my own expense and circulated privately. I thought of a binding in limp leather, possibly blue."

"Sounds swell. Put me down for a copy."

"Thank you. I shall be delighted. It will not be completed, of course, for some years. The subject is too vast."

"I can wait. Say, listen. What I came about was that lucky pig of mine."

"That— I beg your pardon?"

"Little silver ninctobinkus I wear on my bracelet. I've lost it."

"I am sorry."

"Hunted everywhere for it and then suddenly remembered I'd had it last in the bedroom down here when I was dressing. Put it down somewheres and forgot about it."

"These lapses of memory frequently occur."

"Yeah. Well, do you think whoever's got the house now—"

"Miss Leila Yorke, the novelist," said Mr. Cornelius reverently.

"No, really? Is that so? I'm one of her greatest admirers."

"I, also."

"Swell stuff she dishes out. Knocks spots off all competitors."

"Indeed yes," said Mr. Cornelius, though he would not have put it in quite that way.

"Well, do you think she would mind if I just popped up to the bedroom and had a look around?"

"I am sure she would readily give her consent, if she were here, but she has left for London. That, I may say, is the reason for my presence. She asked me to keep an eye on the house. It seems that Miss Yorke received a visit yesterday from a most suspicious character, who tried to insinuate himself into Castlewood on some pretext or other, with the intention, no doubt, of returning later and burgling the place."

"Well, of all the ideas! Sounds cuckoo to me."

"I assure you that sort of thing is frequently done. I was speaking of this man to Mr. Widgeon's cousin, who is in the police and who had had the story from Mr. Widgeon, who had had it from Miss Foster, who had had it from Miss Yorke, and he told me it was a well-known practice of the criminal classes. 'Casing the joint,' it is called, he says. He expressed some chagrin that the exigencies of walking his beat would take him away from Castlewood so that, when the man returned, he would not be there to make what he described as a pinch. He is a most zealous officer."

"I'll bet he is. We want more of his sort around."

"Very true."

"Well, anyway, I'm not casing any joints. All I want is to mosey up to that bedroom and see if my pig's there. I'll prob'ly find I dropped it behind the dressing table or something. Miss Yorke won't mind me doing that?"

"I feel convinced that she would have no objection, but what you suggest is, I fear, impracticable, for before leaving she locked her bedroom door."

"What!"

"On my suggestion," said Mr. Cornelius rather smugly.

Dolly stood silent. Six separate blistering observations had darted into her mind like red-hot bullets, but she remembered in time that she was a lady and did not utter them. Contenting herself with a mere "Oh, is that so? Well, pip-pip." She turned and walked away, giving no indication of the vultures that gnawed at her bosom.

At the corner of the road that led to the station she caught a Number Three omnibus, and this in due season deposited her in Piccadilly Circus. Partly because the day was so fine and partly because she hoped with exercise to still the ferment in her blood, she walked along Piccadilly and turned up Bond Street, and it was as she did this that out of the corner of her eye she observed a well-dressed man behind her.

It has already been stated that the sight of a well-dressed man in her rear often called to Dolly to put into effect the technique which years of practice had bestowed on her. A moment later, she was swooning in his arms, and a moment after that withdrawing the hand that had crept toward his pocket. She had seen his face and knew that there would be little in that pocket to reward the prospector.

"Why, hello, Mr. Widgeon," she said.

11.

Until the moment of impact, Freddie had been in the best of spirits, feeling, like the gentleman in *Oklahoma!* that everything was coming his way. As he started to walk up Bond Street, he was not actually singing "Oh, What a Beautiful Morning!" but it would not have required a great deal of encouragement to induce him to do so. Few things so brace up a young man in springtime as a reconciliation with the girl he loves, and the thought that he and Sally, so recently a couple of sundered hearts, were once more on Romeo-and-Juliet terms would alone have been enough to raise him to the heights and, as we say, bring him to the very brink of bursting into song.

But in addition to this there was the uplifting reflection

that he had in a drawer at Peacehaven scrip of the Silver River Oil and Refinery Corporation which he would shortly be selling for ten thousand pounds and, to set the seal on his happiness, someone at the office, just before he left, had dropped a heavy ledger on the foot of Mr. Jervis, the head clerk, causing him a good deal of pain, for he suffered from corns. In the six months during which he had served under the Shoesmith banner Freddie had come to dislike Mr. Jervis with an intensity quite foreign to his normally genial nature, and he held very strongly the view that the more ledgers that were dropped on him, the better. His only regret was that it had not been a ton of bricks.

All in all, then, conditions, where he was concerned, could scarcely have been improved on, and joy may be said to have reigned supreme.

But the sudden discovery that his arms had become full of totally unforeseen blondes occasioned a sharp drop in his spirits. There had been a time when, if females of this coloring had fallen into his embrace, he would have clasped them to him and asked for more, but that had been in the pre-Sally days. Sally had changed his entire spiritual outlook. And, thinking of her, as he was now doing, he found himself entertaining a chilling speculation as to what she would say if she knew of these goings-on, to be succeeded by the more soothing thought that, being seven miles away in Valley Fields, she would not know of them. And when Dolly spoke and he realized that this was not some passing stranger who had taken a sudden fancy to him, but merely his next-door neighbor Mrs. Molloy, he was quite himself again. His acquaintance with Dolly was not an intimate one, but her husband had introduced them one afternoon and they had occasionally exchanged Good mornings across the fence, so if she had tripped over something and clutched at him for support, there was really nothing in the whole episode that even Emily Post could shake her head at.

When, therefore, she said "Why, hello, Mr. Widgeon," it was with a completely restored equanimity that he replied, "Why, hullo, Mrs. Molloy. Fancy bumping into you."

"Bumping is right. Hope I didn't spoil the sit of your coat. I kind of twisted my ankle."

"Oh, really? Those high heels, what? Always beats me how women can navigate in them. You're all right?"

"Oh, sure, thanks."

"Not feeling faint or anything?"

"A bit sort of shaken up."

"You'd better have a drink."

"Now that's a thought. I could certainly use one."

"In here," said Freddie, indicating the Bollinger bar, outside of which they happened to be standing. "There's no better place, so the cognoscenti inform me."

If at the back of his mind, as they passed through the door, there lurked a shadow of regret that he had not steered his guest to one of the many Bond Street tea shoppes for a quick cup of coffee, instead of giving his patronage to an establishment where, he knew, they charged the earth for an eye-dropperful of alcoholic stimulant, he did not show it. The chivalry of the Widgeons would alone have been enough to keep him from doing that, and when the thought stole into his mind, it was immediately ejected by the reflection that it was to the husband of this woman that he owed the prosperity that in the near future would be his. If a man out of pure goodness of heart has put thousands of pounds in your pocket, the least you can do when you find his wife all shaken from a near fall in Bond Street is to bring her back to midseason form with a beaker of the right stuff, even if her taste inclines to champagne cocktails.

Dolly's taste did, and he bore the blow to a purse ill adapted to the receipt of blows like a Widgeon and a gentleman, not even paling beneath his tan when she drained her first one at a gulp and asked for a refill. Nothing could have been more apparently carefree than his demeanor as he opened the conversation.

"Funny us meeting like this. What are you doing in these parts? Shopping?"

"No, just strolling along. I'm meeting my husband for lunch at Barribault's. We're living there now."

"Really?" said Freddie, impressed. "Nice place."

"Yeah. We're got a very comfortable suite."

"Bit of a change from Valley Fields. It came as quite a surprise when Cornelius told me you had left Castlewood."

"I guess we did move kind of quick, but that's Soapy all over."

"Oh, is it? Who's Soapy?"

"I call Mr. Molloy that. On account of he made his first million in soap. It's a sort of little joke between us."

"I see. Very droll," said Freddie, though he had heard more hilarious pleasantries in his time. "You'll never guess who's got the house now."

"Is it rented again already?"

"Went off right away. New tenant's a terrific celebrity. Leila Yorke, the novelist."

"You don't say? What's she doing in Valley Fields? I was reading a piece in a women's paper, where it said she owned one of those stately homes of England you hear about."

"Yes, Claines Hall, Loose Chippings, down in Sussex.

But she's got the idea of doing a book about the suburbs. Do you read her stuff?"

"I don't, no. I've heard tell of it, but it sounds too mushy for me. What I like is something with plenty of blood and lots of mysterious Chinamen in it."

"Me, too. But you haven't heard the latest. She's changing her act. Her new book's going to be strong and stark and full of grayness and squalor, the sort of thing George Gissing used to write, and she's gone to Valley Fields to get what they call local color. I think myself she's a sap to do it, because her usual bilge sells in vast quantities, and I don't suppose anyone'll buy a copy of this one. Still, there it is. She's got this goofy urge to do bigger and better things, and she means to go through with it."

"Won't her publishers let out a holler?"

"I should imagine a fortissimo one. And poor old Oofy's going to suffer fifty-seven pangs. He put a lot of money in the business, and losing money always cuts him to the quick."

"Oofy?"

"Nobody you know. Fellow clubman of mine. Chap called Prosser."

"Prosser? That name seems to ring a bell. Didn't a Mrs. Prosser have a lot of jewelry snatched not long ago?"

"That's right. Oofy's wife. She turned her back for a moment, and when she looked round the sparklers were gone."

"I read about it in the papers. They think the maid did it, don't they?"

"That's the general idea. When the hue and cry was raised, she had vanished."

"And I must vanish, too, or I'll be late for lunch, and Soapy hates waiting for his eats."

"I'll put you in a taxi," said Freddie, greatly relieved

that no more champagne cocktails were going to flow like water.

He put her in a taxi, and she drove off, waving a slender hand. Freddie waved his in courteous return, and was thinking what a delightful woman Mrs. Molloy was and wishing he had seen more of her during her stay at Castlewood, when his meditations were interrupted by a voice at his elbow, a soprano voice with a nasty tinkle in it.

"Mr. Brigham Young, I believe?" it said, and he jumped perhaps six inches. Sally was standing beside him, and he was quick to note that in her eyes was that unmistakable look which creeps into the eyes of idealistic girls when they see their betrothed helping blondes into taxis and waving after them with, it seems to them, far too much warmheartedness.

"Good Lord, Sally!" he said. "You gave me a start."

"I'm not surprised."

"What on earth are you doing here?"

"I've been seeing Leila Yorke's publishers about her change of plans regarding the next book. Their offices are just round the corner. Didn't you hear them screaming? Well?"

"How do you mean, 'Well?' "

"You would prefer I made myself clearer? All right, then, put it this way. Who was that lady I saw you coming down the street with?"

"Oh, the beazel who was here just now?"

"That is the beazel to whom I refer."

There is probably nothing so stimulating to a young fiancé in circumstances such as these as the knowledge that he has got his story ready and that it will be impossible for the most captious critic to punch holes in it. Where a young man less happily situated would have shuffled his feet and stammered sentences beginning with "Er—,"

Freddie stood firm and foursquare, and his voice, when he spoke, came out as clear and unhesitating as that of Mr. Cornelius when reciting his favorite passage from Sir Walter Scott's "Lady of the Lake."

"That was Mrs. Molloy."

"Ah, a new one."

Freddie's manner became cold and dignified.

"If you mean by that what I think you mean, you're missing your pitch and are very much off on your downbeat. Correct this tendency of yours to allow a diseased imagination to run away with you and make you say things which can only lead to bitter remorse. Ever seen driven snow?"

"I know the sort of snow you mean."

"Well, that's what I'm as pure as. That, I was saying, was Mrs. Molloy, and I was about to add, when you interrupted me, that she is the wife of Thomas G. Molloy, who resided at Castlewood before Miss Yorke took over. She twisted her ankle as she was walking along the street—"

"Lucky she had you at her side."

"She didn't have me at her ruddy side, not the way you mean. If you will be good enough to keep your trap shut for just half a minute, I will explain the circumstances and explain them fully. She was not walking along the street with me, but far otherwise, I was walking along the street, as it might be here, and she was walking along the street, as it might be there, quite distinct and separate, and suddenly she twisted this ankle of which I spoke. I saw her stumble—she was just in front of me—and very naturally grabbed her."

"Ah!"

" 'Ah' does not enter into it. If you see a female, and one to whom you have been formally introduced by her husband, about to take a toss, there is no course open to you but to lend her a hand. Chivalry demands it. So when you accuse me of licentious behavior in the middle of Bond Street, you are, as you will readily appreciate, talking through the back of your foolish little neck."

"I didn't accuse you of licentious behavior."

"You were going to when you got around to it. Well, having grabbed her, I thought she might be feeling faint after her unpleasant experience, so I took her into the Bollinger for a quick tissue restorer. And," said Freddie with feeling, "the prices they charge in that thieves' kitchen are enough to whiten your hair from the roots up. I was the one who was feeling faint when the waiter brought the bad news. I thought for a moment he must have added in the date."

"But it was worth the expense?"

"What do you mean by that?"

"Oh, nothing."

"I should hope not. It's no pleasure to me to pay out large sums, which I can ill afford, for champagne for women who are comparative strangers."

"Then why did you do it?"

Something that was almost a pang shot through Freddie as he thought how silly this girl was going to look in about fifty seconds or so. No man of fine sensibilities can ever really enjoy bathing the woman he loves in confusion and bringing home to her with a wallop what a priceless ass she has been making of herself with her baseless suspicions and cracks about Brigham Young and "new ones," but sometimes it has to be done. One must have discipline. He crushed pity down and spoke.

"I'll tell you why I did it. Because I was under a great obligation to her husband, Thomas G. Molloy, who recently out of pure goodness of heart let me have some oil stock which I shall be selling shortly for a matter of ten thousand quid."

"Freddie!"

"You may well say 'Freddie!' If anything, the word understates it. Yes, those are the facts, and I took the view that as Molloy had done the square thing by me in so stupendous a fashion, the least I could do in return was to lead his stricken wife into the Bollinger and tell the man behind the bar to fill her up, even with champagne cocktails costing a king's ransom, and she knocked back two of them and there was a moment when I thought she was going to order a third."

He had been right in supposing that his revelation of the inside story would have a powerful effect on the party of the second part.

"Oo!" said Sally.

"Ten thousand *pounds!*" said Sally.

"Oh, *Freddie!*" said Sally.

He pressed his advantage like a good general.

"Now perhaps you understand why I mentioned driven snow."

"Of course."

"No more baseless suspicions?"

"Not one."

"In short, sweethearts still?"

"You take the words out of my mouth."

"Then come along to some fairly cheap hostelry, and I'll give you lunch. And while we revel I'll tell you about Kenya and the bit of luck that's shortly going to happen to the coffee industry out there."

The operative word in Freddie's concluding remarks had been the adjective "cheap," so it was not to Barribault's that he escorted Sally for the midday meal. Had he done so, they might have observed Mr. and Mrs. Molloy seated at a table against the wall, in which event the animation of the latter would not have escaped their notice. Dolly, who had depressed her husband over the smoked salmon with a description of her misadventures in Valley Fields, was now, with the chicken in aspic, about to bring the sunshine into his life again.

"It's all right, Soapy," she was saying. "We aren't licked yet."

"Who says so?" inquired Mr. Molloy morosely. The tale to which he had been listening had turned the smoked salmon to ashes in his mouth, and he was not expecting better things of the chicken in aspic.

"Me, that's who, and I'll tell you why. On my way here I ran into young Widgeon in Bond Street, and he told me something that gave me an idea that's going to fix everything. You know the Yorke dame."

Soapy quivered a little.

"We've met," he said in a hushed voice.

"I mean, you know the sort of junk she writes?"

"No, I don't. What do you think I am? A bookworm?"

"Well, it's that mushy stuff that sells like hot dogs at Coney Island, and she's got a million fans over here and in America, too, but I guess she's got fed up with dishing out the marshmallow and chocolate sauce, because her next book's going to be one of those strong, stark things, so Widgeon tells me, quite different from her ordinary boloney."

"So what?" said Mr. Molloy, still morose.

"Well, that's news, isn't it? That's the sort of thing that's going to interest a whole lot of people, isn't it? So what'll seem more natural to her than having *Time* or *Newsweek* or someone—I mean some American magazine, that's got a London office—call her up and say can they send along one of their dames to get the low-down and find out why she's making the switch. So this dame goes down to Castlewood and asks her what the hell and all that, and then she says she needs some photographs of the house, including the bedroom, on account of their readers are always interested in bedrooms, and there you are, we're in."

Mr. Molloy, as has been indicated, was not a very quick-thinking man except when engaged in his professional activities, but even he could see that there was much in what she said. He had been raising a segment of chicken to his lips, and he paused spellbound with the fork in mid-air. He was no longer morose.

"Baby," he said. "I believe you've got it."

"You can say that again. Can't slip up, far as I can see. I'll call her after lunch and make the date."

A flaw in the setup occurred to Mr. Molloy.

"But you haven't got a camera."

"That's all right," said Dolly. "I'll pick one up at Self-ridge's this afternoon."

12.

While entertaining Sally at lunch (shepherd's pie and an apple dumpling) at a pub he knew around the corner, Freddie had enjoined strict secrecy upon her in the matter of the Silver River Oil and Refinery Corporation, just as Mr. Molloy when letting him have that stock had enjoined it on him. Mr. Molloy, he explained, was planning to buy up all the outstanding shares and very naturally wanted to secure them at a low price, which he would not be able to do if people went around shooting their heads off about what a terrific thing it was. The principle, he said, was the same as when someone gives you a tip on a fifty-to-one outsider straight from the mouth of the stable cat and tells you to keep it under your hat so as not to shorten the odds. He was conscious as he spoke of a slight feeling of guilt as he remembered that he had not pursued this sealed-lips policy when chatting with Mr. Cornelius a few days ago, but too late to worry about that now, and anyway Mr. Cornelius, immersed as he was in house agenting and rabbits, was not likely to spread the news.

So when Sally rejoined Leila Yorke and started homeward with her in the car, it was not of the coming ten thousand pounds that she spoke, but of the Pen and Ink Club luncheon and Miss Yorke's speech.

"How did it go?" she asked. "Were you in good voice?"

"Oh, yes."

"What did you say?"

"The usual applesauce."

"How many gargoyles were there?"

"About a million."

"What were their hats like?"

"Nothing on earth," said Leila Yorke.

Her manner was not responsive, but Sally persevered.

"I saw Mr. Saxby."

"Oh?"

"He took it big, as anticipated. So did Popgood and Grooly. At least, Grooly. I didn't see Popgood. Grooly turned ashy pale, and said you ought to have your head examined."

"Oh?"

"I left him ringing up Mr. Prosser, to tell him the bad news."

"Oh, yes?" said Leila Yorke, and she relapsed into a silence that lasted till the end of the journey.

Sally, as she put the car away, felt concerned. Taciturnity on this scale was quite foreign to her usually exuberant employer. It might, of course, be merely the normal letdown which results from sitting through a women's luncheon, but she felt it went deeper than that. Even after two hours of looking at members of the Pen and Ink Club, Leila Yorke ought to be cheerier than this.

It seemed to her that what was needed here was a nice cup of tea. She had never herself attended one of these literary luncheons, but she knew people who had and had gathered from them that all the material, as opposed to intellectual, food you got at them was half a tepid grapefruit with a cherry in it, some sort of hashed chicken embedded in soggy pastry and a stewed pear. No doubt Leila Yorke's despondency was due to malnutrition, and this could be corrected with tea and plenty of buttered toast. She prepared these lifesaving ingredients and put them on a tray and took them out into the garden, where Miss Yorke was sitting gazing before her with what in her books she liked to describe as unseeing eyes.

The listlessness with which she accepted the refreshment emboldened Sally to speak. In the months which she had spent at Claines Hall she had become very fond of Leila Yorke, and she hated to see her in this mood of depression.

"What's the trouble?" she asked abruptly.

She was aware that she was exposing herself to a snub. It would have been quite open to the other, thus addressed by a humble secretary, to raise a cold eyebrow and reply that she failed to understand her meaning or, more probably, seeing that it was Miss Yorke, to ask her what the hell she thought she was talking about. But the question had come at a moment when the novelist needed to unburden her mind. There is something about grapefruit with a cherry in it, hashed chicken in pastry and stewed pears that breaks down reserve and inspires confidences.

She did not raise her eyebrows. She said, quite simply,

as if she was glad Sally had asked her that, "I'm worried about Joe."

Sally knew who Joe was, Leila Yorke's mystery husband, who had passed into the discard some years previously. There had been occasional references to him during her tenure of office, the latest only yesterday, and she had often wondered what manner of man he had been. She always pictured him as a large, dominant character with keen eyes and a military mustache, for she could not imagine anything less hardy entering into matrimony with so formidable a woman. Yes, big and keen-eyed and strong and, of course, silent. He would have had to be that, married to someone as voluble as Miss Yorke.

"Oh, yes?" was all she found herself able to say. It was not the best of observations, but it seemed to encourage her companion to proceed.

"I saw him this afternoon."

This time Sally's response was even briefer. She said, "Oh?"

"Yes," said Leila Yorke, "there he was. He looked just the same as he always did. Except," she added, "for a bald spot. I always told him his hair would go, if he didn't do daily hair drill."

Sally had no comment to make on the bald spot. She merely held her breath.

"Gave me a shock, seeing him suddenly like that."

On the point of saying she didn't wonder, Sally checked herself. Silence, she felt, was best. There was something in all this a little reminiscent of a deathbed confession, and one does not interrupt deathbed confessions.

"Hadn't seen him for three years. He was still living with his mother then."

Sally's interest deepened. So Joe had gone back to his mother, had he. This was, she knew, a common procedure with wives, but rarer with husbands. She found herself revising the mental picture she had made. A man like the Joe she had imagined would have taken his gun and gone off to the Rocky Mountains to shoot grizzly bears.

"That mother of his! Snakes!" said Miss Yorke unexpectedly.

"Snakes?" said Sally, surprised. She felt that a monosyllable would not break the spell, and she wanted to have this theme developed. She was convinced that the word had not been a mere exclamation. A strongly moved woman might ejaculate "Great Snakes!" but surely not "Snakes!" alone.

"She kept them," explained Miss Yorke. "She was in vaudeville—Herpina, the Snake Queen—and she used them in her act. When," she added with some bitterness, "she could get bookings, which wasn't often." She sighed, or, rather, said "Oh, hell!" which was her way of heaving a sigh. "Did I ever tell you about my married life, Sally?"

"No, never. I knew you had been married, of course."

"You'd have liked Joe. Everybody did. I loved him. Still do, blast it. His trouble was he was so weak. Just a rabbit who couldn't say 'Boo!' to a goose."

Sally knew that the number of rabbits capable of saying "Boo!" to geese is very limited, but she did not point this out. She was too busy making further revisions in the mental portrait.

"So when his mother, one of the times when she was 'resting,' suggested that she should come and live with us, he hadn't the nerve to tell her she wasn't wanted and that the little woman would throw a fit if she set foot across the threshold. He just said 'Fine!' And as he hadn't the nerve to tell me what he'd done, the first inkling I got of what was happening was when I came home all tired out from a heavy day at the office—I was a sob sister then on one of the evening papers—and found her in my favorite chair, swigging tea and fondling her snakes. A nice homecoming that was, and so I told Joe when I got him alone. He had the gall to say that he had thought she would be such nice company for me when he was away on tour."

"Was he an actor?"

"Of a sort. He never got a part in the West End, but he did all right in the provinces, and he was always going off to play juvenile leads in Wolverhampton and Peebles and places of that kind. So Mother and snakes dug themselves into the woodwork, and that," said Miss Yorke, again unexpectedly, "was how I got my start."

Sally blinked.

"How do you mean?"

"Perfectly simple. Everyone who's on a paper is always going to do a novel when he gets time, and I had often thought of having a bash at one, because if you're a sob sister, you accumulate a whole lot of material. This was where I saw my opportunity of buckling down to it. Instead of spending my evenings listening to Mother saying how big she had gone at the Royal, Wigan, and how it was only jealousy in high places that had kept her from working her act in London, I shut myself up in my room and wrote my first novel. It was *Heather o' the Hills*. Ever read it?"

"Of course."

"Pure slush, but it was taken by Popgood and Grooly, and didn't do too badly, and they sent the sheets over to Singleton Brothers in New York, who turn out books like sausages and don't care how bad they are, so long as they run to eighty thousand words. They chucked it into the sausage machine and twiddled the handle and darned if it wasn't one of the biggest sellers they had that season.

What's known as a sleeper. And they asked me to come to New York and lend a hand with the publicity, autograph copies in department stores and all that. Well, Joe was still on tour with half a dozen more towns to play, and I thought I'd only be over there a few weeks, so I went. And of course the damned book was bought for pictures and I had to go out to Hollywood to work on it, and when I'd been there a couple of months I sent Joe five thousand dollars and told him this looked like being a long operation so he must come and join me. And what do you think?"

"What?"

"He wrote back thanking me for the five grand and saying he couldn't make it, as his mother didn't want him to leave her. Said she had palpitations or something. It made me so mad that I did what I can see now was the wrong thing. I said to myself, All right, Joe, if you can do without me, I can do without you, and I stayed on in America six solid years. By that time I suppose we had both taken it for granted that the marriage was washed up."

"You didn't get a divorce?"

"Never occurred to me. I'm a one-man woman. I wouldn't have wanted to marry anyone, after having Joe. I just let things drift. Three years ago I ran into him in the street and we talked for a while. I asked him if he was all right for money, and he said he was. He had written a play that was being taken on tour, he said, and I wished him luck and he wished me luck, and I asked after his mother and he said she was living with him and still had the snakes, and I said that was fine, and I came away and cried all night."

It cost Sally an effort to break the silence which followed. Speech seemed intrusive.

"And you saw him again today?"

"Yes," said Leila Yorke. "He was one of the waiters at the luncheon."

Sally gasped. "A waiter!"

"That's what I said. They always get in a lot of extra waiters for these affairs, and he was one of them."

"But that must mean—"

"—that he's absolutely broke. Of course it does, and I've got to find him. But how the devil do you find an extra waiter in the whole of London?"

Inside the house, as they wrestled with this problem, the telephone began to ring.

"Answer it, will you, Sally," said Leila Yorke wearily. "If it's that man Cornelius, say I'm dead."

"It's somebody from *Time*," said Sally, returning. "They want to interview you about your new book."

"Tell them to go and— No, better not. Male or female?"

"Female."

"All right, tell the pest she can come tomorrow at five," said Leila Yorke. "That gives me twenty-four hours. Perhaps by then she'll have been run over by a bus or something."

13.

Tuesday began well for Freddie's cousin George. Leaning over the Nook-Peacehaven fence as the other fed his rabbits, he not only sold Mr. Cornelius two of the five-shilling tickets for the forthcoming concert in aid of the Policemen's Orphanage but received from him the information that Castlewood was now occupied by a famous female novelist, a piece of news that stirred him like a police whistle. All female novelists, he knew, were wealthy beyond the dreams of avarice, and he was convinced that if this one were to be properly approached, with just the right organ note in the voice, business could not fail to result. Before starting out on his beat, accordingly, he gave his uniform a lick with the clothes brush, said "Mi, mi," once or twice to himself in an undertone and, clumping over to Castlewood in his official boots, rang the bell.

Sally opened the door to him, and he gazed at her with undisguised admiration. Being betrothed to a charming girl who was something secretarial in a shipping office, a Miss Jennifer Tibbett, he took, of course, only an academic interest in the appearance of such others of her sex as he encountered, but his eye was not dimmed and he was able to see that here was something rather special in the way of nymphery. He approved wholeheartedly of this exhibit's trim little figure, her slightly tiptilted nose, her copper-colored hair and the blue eyes that gazed into his. The last-named seemed to him to be shining like twin stars, as he believed the expression was, and he was not mistaken in thinking so. Sally, while preparing breakfast for her employer, had been meditating on Freddie and how much she loved him, and thoughts of that nature always give the eyes a sparkle.

"Oh, hullo," he said. "I mean what ho. I mean good morning."

The subject being one that he considered too sacred to be discussed with cousins, especially cousins who, he knew from experience, had a tendency to greet his tales of love with uncouth guffaws, Freddie had not mentioned Sally to George. He shrank from having his idyll soiled by ribald criticism, and something told him that ribald was what George would inevitably be if informed that he, Freddie, had found the real thing at last. Intimate with the last of the Widgeons since their kindergarten days, George knew how volatile were his affections. It had, indeed, though Sally was not aware of it, been he who at that cocktail party had uttered those words about Piccadilly Circus and Hyde Park Corner which she had found so disturbing.

All that George knew of Sally, therefore, was what he had learned from Mr. Cornelius—to wit, that Miss Yorke in her descent on Valley Fields had been accompanied by a secretary. A rather attractive girl, the house agent had said, and to George, drinking her in, this seemed an understatement of the first water. She was, in his opinion, a grade-A pippin, and he could see Freddie, if and when he made her acquaintance, straightening his tie, shooting his cuffs and, like the horse to which allusion was made earlier, saying "Ha, ha" among the trumpets.

"I say," he proceeded, "do take a lenient view of this unwarrantable intrusion, as I've sometimes heard it called. I live next door, and I thought it would be neighborly if I looked in and passed the time of day."

"Oh?" Sally's smile was of such a caliber that, if he had not been armored by his great love for Miss Tibbett, it would have gone through him like a bullet through blancmange. As it was, it made him totter for a moment. "You're Freddie's cousin, the policeman. He was telling me about you."

George was conscious of a feeling of awed respect for his kinsman's enterprise. He had always known that he was a quick worker, never letting the grass grow beneath his feet in his dealings with the young and beautiful, but in not only introducing himself to but in getting to be on such familiar terms with a girl who hadn't been around for more than about twenty-four hours, he had, in George's opinion, excelled himself. "Freddie" already! Quick service, that. Why, in his own case it had been a matter of three weeks before he had got past the surname stage. It was a gift, of course, and Freddie had it and he hadn't.

"That's right," he said. "Great chap, Freddie. Always reminds me of one of those fellows who bound on stage with a racquet at the beginning of a play and say 'Tennis, anyone?' "

Sally stiffened.

"He isn't in the least like that."

She spoke coldly, and George saw that he had said the wrong thing. He hastened to correct himself.

"I only meant he's not a beefy bird like me, but slim and graceful and all that."

"Yes, you're right there."

"Svelte, shall we call him?"

"If you like."

"Fine," said George, relieved. "We pencil Freddie in as svelte. And now, for I shall have to be popping off in a moment to discourage the local crime wave, could I have a word with Miss Leila Yorke?"

"She's breakfasting in bed. Can I give her a message?"

George fingered his chin.

"Well, it might work that way," he said dubiously, "but I had hoped to come face to face with her and give her the old personality, if you understand what I mean. You see, I'm trying to sell tickets for the annual concert in aid of the Policemen's Orphanage, to be held at the Oddfellows Hall in Ogilvy Street next month, and my chances of success are always much brighter if I can get hold of the prospect by the coat button and give him—or, as in this case, her—all that stuff about supporting a charitable organization which is not only most deserving in itself but is connected with a body of men to whom he—or she—as a householder will be the first to admit that he or she owes the safety of his or her person and the tranquillity of his or her home—in other words, to cut a long story short and get right down to the nub, the police. There's a lot more of it, but you will have got the idea."

"Yes. I've got it. Did you think all that up by yourself?"

"Good Lord, no. It's written out for us by the big shots, and we memorize it. All over Valley Fields and adjoining suburbs at this moment a hundred flatties are intoning it in the ears of the rate-paying public."

"It must sound heavenly. Will it be a good concert?"

"Sensational."

"How much are the tickets?"

"They vary. The five-shilling ones are five shillings, the half-crown ones half a crown, the two-shilling ones—"

"Two shillings?"

"You guessed it right off," said George, regarding her with an increase of his previous admiration, as if stunned by this blending of brains and beauty. "And the shilling ones are a shilling and the sixpenny ones sixpence. The last named, those at a tanner, I don't recommend very highly, because all they draw is standing room. They are traditionally reserved for the canaille and the under-privileged, the poor slobs who can't afford anything better."

Sally had made a discovery.

"You do talk beautifully," she said.

"I do, rather," George agreed.

"And just like Freddie."

"Better than Freddie, I should have said. Well, will you toddle off like a dear little soul and see if you can work Miss Yorke up to the five-bob standard? A woman of her eminence ought to be in the first three rows."

Sally went upstairs and found Leila Yorke sipping tea and looking moody. Her air was that of one who is thinking of extra waiters.

"Did I hear the front doorbell?" she asked.

"Yes, it was a caller."

"Cornelius?"

"Not this time. It was Freddie's cousin George, the cop.

He's selling tickets for the concert in aid of the Police-men's Orphanage."

"Oh, a touch?"

"On a very modest scale. Ten bob will cover it, and you will be supporting a charitable organization which is not only most deserving in itself—"

"Oh, all right. Look in my bag. On the dressing table."

Leila Yorke had spoken listlessly, but now she suddenly sat up and became animated.

"Did you say this bird was a policeman?"

"Complete with helmet and regulation boots. Why?"

"Wouldn't a policeman know all about private eyes?"

"Oh! You mean—?"

"To look for Joe. Go back and ask him if he can recommend somebody for the job."

It was an idea, but to Sally's mind not a very good one.

"Do you think a private detective could do anything? I know they make inquiries and all that, but wouldn't it be rather like looking for a needle in a haystack?"

"Well, that's what private eyes are for. Go and ask him. I've got to find Joe, and this is the only way."

"I suppose it is," said Sally, and she returned to the front steps, where George was standing like a large blue statue, thinking, apparently of absolutely nothing, unless, of course, as it may well have been, his mind was on Miss Jennifer Tibbett. Tapped on the arm and hearing the words "Hi, officer!" he came out of his coma and the light of hope flashed into his face.

"Any luck?"

"Two of the five-bob."

"You're terrific! Was it a fearful struggle? Did you have to twist her arm?"

"Oh, no, she was a cheerful giver. Well, fairly cheerful.

She's a bit down at the moment because she's lost her husband."

George clicked his tongue sympathetically.

"I say, rather a bad show, that. Enough to give any woman the pip. Not but what we've all of us got to go some time. What is it they say all flesh is as? Grass, isn't it?"

"Oh, he isn't dead, he's an extra waiter."

"I'm not sure I quite got that. An extra what?"

Sally explained the position of affairs, and George said Oh, he saw now. For a moment, he added, he had not completely grasped the gist.

"And she asked me to ask you," said Sally, "if you knew any private eyes."

"You mean shamuses?"

"That's right."

"I don't, and I don't want to. Frightful bounders, all of them, from what I've heard. Always watching husbands and wives and trying to get the necessary evidence. We of the force look down on them like anything. Does Miss Yorke want to scoop one in to try and find her husband?"

"That's the idea."

"He'll have his work cut out for him."

"So I told her."

"He'll be looking for a needle in a haystack."

"I said that, too."

"Well, I wish I could help you. I'll tell you what I think her best plan would be. She ought to ask her solicitor."

"Why, of course. A solicitor would probably know dozens of private detectives."

"I think so. Solicitors always have oodles of shady work to be done—documents stolen from rival firms, heirs kidnaped, wills pinched and destroyed, and so on. Trot along and put it up to her. And now, if you'll excuse me," said George, "I must be buzzing off on my official duties, or heaven knows what the denizens of Valley Fields will be getting up to in my absence. Awfully nice to have seen you."

Sally returned to Leila Yorke, who had finished her breakfast and was enjoying one of her mild cigars.

"He says he doesn't know any private eyes, but he thinks a solicitor would."

"I wonder."

"It's worth trying."

"I suppose so. All right, go and see Johnny Shoesmith."

"Very well. I'd better wait till the afternoon. There are a lot of supplies to be got in, and if I'm not here to cook lunch for you, you'll try to do an omelet and make a frightful hash of it. Remember last time? I can't think why you never learned to cook. Didn't you have to get your own meals when you were a sob sister?"

"Me? You are speaking of the time when I was young and beautiful and men lined up in queues to feed me. Your Freddie's Uncle Rodney alone was good for six or seven dinners a week. And when I married, Joe did the cooking. He could cook anything, that boy. We had a little flat in Prince of Wales's Mansions, Battersea, and every night—"

A tear stole into Leila Yorke's eye, and Sally left the room hastily. Taking her shopping bag, she went out into Mulberry Grove and met George, who was emerging from the gate of Peacehaven. He had postponed his grappling with the criminal element of Valley Fields in order to return home and get his cigarettes, one, or possibly more, of which he hoped to be able to smoke when the sergeant's eye was not on him.

"Hullo," he said. "We meet again."

"We do," said Sally. "I'm going shopping. Oh, by the

way, did you find your friend when you got back yester-day?"

George cocked an inquiring eye.

"What friend would that be?"

"I only caught a glimpse of her as I went by in the car. A tallish, fair girl. She was leaning on the gate of Peace-haven."

George's face cleared.

"Oh, ah, yes. I know the girl you mean. I met her and we chatted of this and that. But she was a friend of Fred-die's, not of mine. I had never seen her before in my life. She said she had come to see Freddie and say Hello, by which I took her to mean pick up the threads and all that sort of thing. Well, pip-pip once more," said George, and with a courteous salute he went on his way.

14.

The day which had turned out so well for Freddie's cousin George had proved less enjoyable for Mr. Shoesmith of Lincoln's Inn Fields. At breakfast a usually meticulous cook had served up to him boiled eggs which should have been taken from the saucepan at least a minute earlier and, not content with this tort or misdemeanor, had scorched the toast to the consistency of leather. At lunch at his club, the Demosthenes, he had been cornered by old Mr. Lucas-Gore, whose conversation was always a bleating mélange of anecdotes about Henry James, an author in whom the solicitor's interest had never been anything but tepid. Toward the middle of the afternoon the weather had become close and oppressive, with thunder threatening. And at four o'clock Leila Yorke's secretary had appeared, babbling of private detectives.

A wholesome awe of Leila Yorke, bred in him from the days of his youth, had kept him from throwing the girl out on her ear, as he had wished to do, but he had got rid of her as quickly as possible, and scarcely had she gone when his daughter Myrtle arrived, interrupting him at a moment when he had hoped to be free to attend to the tangled affairs of Freddie's uncle, Lord Blicester, who was having his annual trouble with the income tax authorities. It was almost, Mr. Shoesmith felt, as if Providence were going out of its way to persecute him, and he was reminded of the case of Job, who had been the victim of a somewhat similar series of misfortunes.

Myrtle was not looking her sunniest. Her eyes smoldered, her lips were drawn in a tight line and her general aspect resembled that of the thunderclouds which were banking up in the sky outside. She was a human replica of one of those V-shaped depressions extending over the greater part of the United Kingdom south of the Hebrides which are such a feature of the English summer, and Mr. Shoesmith gazed at her wanly. Knowing her moods, he could recognize the one now gripping her. She had a grievance, and experience had taught him that when she had a grievance she sat and talked for hours, taking up time which could have been more profitably employed on lucrative work such as the tangled affairs of Lord Blicester. Wrenched from these, he felt like a dog deprived of a bone.

"Ah, Myrtle," he said, resisting a temptation to strike his child with the Blicester dossier. "Take a chair. Unpleasant weather. How is Alexander?"

He was not really interested in the health of his son-in-law, whose only merit in his eyes was his colossal wealth, but one must start a conversation somehow.

Myrtle, who had already taken a chair and looked, to her father's anxious eyes, as if she had glued herself to it, sat for a space breathing tempestuously through her nose. Her resemblance to a thundercloud had become more noticeable.

"Alexander is very upset."

"I'm not surprised."

"Why, have you heard?"

"Heard what?"

"About that Leila Yorke woman."

"What about her?"

"So you haven't heard. Then why did you say you weren't surprised that Alexander is upset?"

What had led Mr. Shoesmith to do so had been his familiarity with Oofy's habit of starting the day with a morning hangover, but he felt that it would be injudicious and possibly dangerous to put this into words. He replied that he was aware how delicate his son-in-law's digestion was.

"Eaten something that disagreed with him?" he asked with as much sympathy as he could muster, which was not a great deal.

Myrtle's breathing took on a snorting sound.

"My dear father, you don't suppose I came all this way to talk about Alexander's digestion. He's upset about this frightful business of Leila Yorke. I think she must have gone off her head. You know Alexander owns the majority stock in Popgood and Grooly, who publish her books?"

"Yes, you told me. A very sound firm, from all I hear. Bessie alone—"

"Who is Bessie?"

Mr. Shoesmith assumed the manner which Freddie

Widgeon disliked so much, his dry, put-you-in-your-place manner.

"An old friend of mine who writes under the pseudonym of Leila Yorke. She was Bessie Binns when I first knew her, and it is pardonable of me, I think, to refer to her by her real name. But if you would prefer that I do not do so, your wishes are law. I was about to say when you interrupted me—we were speaking, if you remember, of the financial stability of the publishing house of Popgood and Grooly—that Leila Yorke alone must be worth a good many thousands of pounds to them annually."

A curious sound which might have been a hollow laugh escaped Myrtle.

"Yes, because up to now she has written the sort of . . ." She hesitated for a word.

"Bilge?" suggested Mr. Shoesmith.

"If you like to put it that way. I was going to say the sort of horrible sentimental stuff that appeals to women. There isn't an author in England who has a bigger library public. Women worship her."

Mr. Shoesmith cackled like a hen, his way of chuckling.

"I wonder what they would think of her if they met her. She certainly isn't like her work. But why do you say 'up to now'?"

"Because she's planning to do something quite different with her next book. Her secretary called on Mr. Grooly yesterday and told him that the novel she's working on now is going to be gray and stark and grim, like George Gissing."

"A fine writer."

"I dare say; but he didn't sell. Imagine the effect this will have on her public. She'll lose every reader she's got."

"So that is why Alexander is upset?"

"Isn't it natural that he should be? It means thousands

of pounds out of his pocket. I was in the room when Mr. Grooly telephoned to tell him the news, and he turned ashy pale."

An improvement, Mr. Shoesmith thought. He had never admired his son-in-law's complexion. Owing to a too-pronounced fondness for champagne, Oofy had always been redder than the rose, and Mr. Shoesmith preferred the male cheek to be more damask.

"Has she written the book?" he asked.

"She's thinking it out. She has gone down to the suburbs to get local color."

"It may turn out to be very good."

"But it won't be Leila Yorke. Can't you understand? When people see the name Leila Yorke on a novel, they expect Leila Yorke stuff, and if they don't get it, they drop her like a hot coal. How would you like it if you bought a book you thought was about company law and found it was a murder mystery?"

"I'd love it," said Mr. Shoesmith frankly.

"Well, Leila Yorke's public won't. This book will kill her stone dead. She won't have a reader left."

"I don't suppose she cares. She's been making twenty thousand pounds a year for the last fifteen years and saving most of it. It seems to me it's entirely her own affair if she spurns Popgood and Grooly's gold and decides to go in for art for art's sake. I don't understand the Popgood and Grooly agitation. If they don't want to publish the thing, they don't have to."

"But they do. She's got a contract for six more books."

"Then what on earth do you expect me to do?" said Mr. Shoesmith, trying not to speak petulantly but missing his objective by a wide margin. The conflict between Lord Blicester and the income tax authorities presented several points of nice legal interest, and he was longing to get back to them. Not for the first time he was regretting that his daughter had not married someone with a job out in, say, the Federated Malay States, where leave to come to England is given only about once every five years. "If she has a contract—"

"I've brought it with me." Myrtle was fumbling in her bag. "I thought you might be able to find something in it which would prevent her doing this insane thing."

"I doubt it," said Mr. Shoesmith, taking the document. He skimmed through it with a practiced eye and handed it back. "I thought so. Not a word even remotely specifying any particular type of book."

"But isn't it implied?"

"Isn't what implied?"

"That she's got to do the sort of thing she has always done."

"Certainly not. You don't imply conditions in contracts, you state them in black and white."

"Do you mean to say that if Agatha Christie had a contract with her publisher—"

"No doubt she has."

"—that she could suddenly decide to turn in something like *Finnegans Wake?*"

"Certainly."

"And the publisher would have to publish it?"

"If he had so contracted."

"That is the law?"

"It is."

"Then the law's idiotic."

"Dickens put it better. He said it was a hass. But even if you and he are right, there is nothing to be done about it."

Myrtle rose, a thing which Mr. Shoesmith had begun to

feel that she was incapable of doing. A new animation came into his manner.

"Are you leaving me?" he asked, trying to keep exhilaration out of his voice.

Myrtle gathered up bag and umbrella. Her face was set and determined.

"Yes, I am going to Valley Fields."

"Odd spot to choose for a jaunt. Why not Surbiton?"

"This is not a jaunt, as you call it. Leila Yorke is living in Valley Fields, and I am going to see her and talk to her."

"You think that that will accomplish something desirable?"

"I hope so."

"I wonder. From what I know of Bessie, she is not a woman lightly to be turned from her purpose. Still, 'try anything once' is always a good motto. Goodbye, my dear. Nice of you to have looked in. Give my regards to Alexander," said Mr. Shoesmith, and he was deep in the affairs of Lord Blicester, almost before the door had closed.

Dolly, meanwhile, down at Castlewood with her notebook and her new camera, was finding her hostess charming. Leila Yorke, though she raged, like the heathen, furiously and muttered things better left unmuttered when one of them announced his or her intention of coming to see her, was always at her best with interviewers. She put them at their ease—not that Dolly needed that—and made a social success of the thing, feeling, for she was essentially a kindly woman, that it was not the fault of these children of unmarried parents if their editors told them to go and make pests of themselves. In her sob sister days she had had to do a good deal of interviewing herself, and she could sympathize with them.

Dolly she found unexpectedly congenial. Hard things had often been said of the light of Soapy Molloy's life by those who knew her—Chimp Twist, trading as J. Sheringham Adair, private investigator, was always particularly vehement when her name came up in the course of conversation—but she was unquestionably good company, and Leila Yorke took to her from the start. They roamed the parklike grounds of Castlewood in perfect amity, and she was delighted with the intelligent girl's attitude toward the change she was proposing to make in her approach to the life literary. Dolly left no room for doubt that she thoroughly approved of it.

"Onward and upward with the arts," she said. "Can't always be giving them the same old boloney. Look at a guy I . . ." She paused. She had been about to say "know" but felt it would be more prudent to substitute a less compromising verb. "Look at a guy I heard about through working on papers, like you do hear about all sorts when you work on papers. Fellow named Easy-Pickings McGee, who had a business in Cicero, outside Chicago. Used to stick up filling stations and drugstores and all like that and made a good enough living for years, and then one morning he says to himself, 'I'm through with this small-time stuff. I've gotten into a rut. I ought to be striving for something bigger.' So he goes right out and sticks up a bank and from that moment never looked back. Got his own gang now, and is one of the most highly thought-of operators in Cook County. I know for a fact—because someone told me," she added hastily—"that he has fifty-six suits of clothes, all silk lined and custom made, and a different pair of shoes for every day in the year. Well, there you are. Ambition pays off."

Leila Yorke said she had an idea that Horatio Alger had written a story of success on much these lines, and Dolly said "Mebbe." She had not, she explained, read very deeply in her Horatio Alger.

"But you see what I mean. You're in the same kind of a spot he was. You're doin' all right for a mountain girl, as the song says, but you feel the time has come to show 'em what you can do when you spit on your hands and go to it. You just carry on, honey, the way you want, and if anyone makes a holler, tell 'em to drop dead."

This so exactly chimed in with Leila Yorke's sentiments that she beamed on her visitor and cordially allowed herself to be photographed in a variety of attitudes, though if there was one thing she disliked more than another about these interviews, it was being propped up against something and told to smile. And it was as she relaxed from the last pose—leaning with one hand on the birdbath and gazing brightly over her left shoulder— that the leaden sky, which had hitherto not spoken, suddenly burst into sound. Thunder roared, lightning flashed, and rain began to descend in the manner popularized by Niagara Falls.

Dolly, being nearest to the French window of the living room, was the first to reach it, with Leila Yorke a close second. They stood looking out on the downpour.

"This realm, this England!" said Miss Yorke bitterly.

"Yeah," Dolly agreed. "I'll bet that guy who returned here after wandering on some foreign strand kicked himself squarely in the derrière for being such a chump as to come back. I wish I had the umbrella concession for this darned country. Well, seeing we're indoors and no chance of getting anything more in the garden, how about some interiors? Tell you what I'd like to have," said Dolly, struck with an idea, "and that's a shot of your bedroom. Kind of intimate, sort of. Mind if I go up?"

"Certainly. Room on the left at the top of the stairs."

"I'll find it," said Dolly, and at this moment the front doorbell rang.

With an impatient grunt, for this, she supposed, could only be Mr. Cornelius again, Leila Yorke went to answer it, and Dolly, about to follow and mount the stairs that led to Eldorado, was frozen in mid-step by a voice she had no difficulty in recognizing.

"Miss Yorke?" said the voice. "Can I come in and speak to you on a matter of importance? My name is Mrs. Alexander Prosser."

It is inevitable, as we pass through life, that we meet individuals whom we are reluctant to meet again. Sometimes it is the way they clear their throats that offends us, sometimes the noise they make when drinking soup, or possibly they remind us of relatives whom we wish to forget. It was for none of these fanciful reasons that Dolly preferred not to encounter Myrtle Prosser, and for an instant, knowing that she was on her way in and that ere long there would be a recognition scene which could not fail to be painful, she stood transfixed. Then life returned to the rigid limbs, and she was her resourceful self again. There was a whirring sound as she dashed back into the living room, dashed through the French windows and dashed across the garden and over the fence that separated it from that of Peacehaven.

In Peacehaven, if the back door was not locked, she would find the hide-out which on an occasion like this is so essential to the criminal classes.

15.

Standing before the mirror in his bedroom at Peacehaven, George was brushing his ginger hair with unusual care and wondering whether a drop of Scalpo, the lotion that lends a luster, would not give it just that little extra something which stamps the man of distinction. He was wearing a blue flannel suit with an invisible stripe, and his shoes, so different from regulation boots, shone with the light that never was on land or sea, for he had wangled a night off from his official duties and was taking Jennifer Tibbett to dinner and a theater. It was not often that he was able to do this, and his heart was light and his attitude toward all created things kindly and benevolent. If a burglar were to enter Peacehaven at this moment, he felt, he would give him a drink and a ham sandwich and help him pack his sack.

And by one of those odd coincidences he became aware, just as this thought floated into his mind, that a burglar had entered Peacehaven. Down below, somebody had sneezed, and as Freddie would not be back from his office for at least another half hour this sneezer could only be an unauthorized intruder. Replacing the hairbrush on the dressing table, he went down, the milk of human kindness still surging within him, to play the host and was interested to discover in the living room the golden-haired young woman with whom he had had such a stimulating conversation on the previous day. The sight of her increased the respect he always felt for Freddie's ability to fascinate the other sex. Wherein lay his cousin's magic, he could not say, but he certainly acted on the beazels like catnip on cats. This girl obviously could not keep away from him, drawn as with a magnet. Like the moth and the candle, thought George.

"Oh, hullo," he said. "You popped in again? Want to see Freddie? He ought to be arriving shortly. Stick around, is my advice."

"I will, if you don't mind," said Dolly, fighting down the womanly tremor she always felt when in the presence of the police. She eyed him closely, taking in with some bewilderment the flannel suit, the neat red tie and the shining shoes. "You'll excuse me asking," she said, "but what are you made up for?"

"Just gentleman, English, ordinary, one. I'm off duty."

"That's good," said Dolly, breathing more freely. "I mean for you."

"Yes, it's nice to get away from the old grind once in a while. One needs an occasional respite, or the machine breaks down. Ask any well-known Harley Street physician."

"Who's attending to all the murders?"

"Oh, a bunch of the other boys. They'll carry on all right in my absence. I say," said George, making a discovery which Sherlock Holmes certainly and Scotland Yard in all probability would have made earlier, "you're wet."

His observant eye had not deceived him. The trip from Castlewood to Peacehaven, though not a long one, had been long enough for the rain to get in some pretty solid work, and Dolly had been exposed to it for some unforeseen extra moments owing to falling while climbing the fence. George, who was given to homely similes, thought she looked like a drowned rat. Being also somewhat deficient in tact, he said so, and Dolly bridled.

"Drowned rats to you, with knobs on," she said coldly. "You're no oil painting yourself."

"Why, yes, if you put it that way," said George, "I suppose you're right. Well, unless you want to get a nasty cold in the head, you'd better change."

"Into what?"

"Ah, that's rather the problem, isn't it. Into, as you say, what? I know," said George, inspired. "Nip up to Freddie's room and swipe a pair of his pajamas. I'd offer you mine, but they wouldn't fit you. Bedroom slippers can also be provided. Come along up, and I'll show you. There you are," he said a few moments later. "Pajamas and slippers, precisely as envisaged. Your kit'll be dry by the time you're ready to leave. Anything else I can do for you in the way of hospitality?"

"Will it be okay for me to make myself a cup of hot coffee?"

"Perfectly okay. This is Liberty Hall. You'll find all the

ingredients in the kitchen. And now I'm afraid I must tear myself away. I'm taking my betrothed to dinner," said George, and with a kindly smile removed himself, feeling like a Boy Scout. Doing this little act of kindness had just put the finishing touch on the mood of yeasty happiness that always uplifted him when he was going to watch Jennifer Tibbett eat lamb cutlets and mashed potatoes. It made him feel worthier of her.

His departure left Dolly a prey to mixed emotions. She liked George as a man and found him an entertaining companion, but she could not forget that for all his suavity and the sparkle of his conversation he represented the awful majesty of the Law and, were he to learn of her activities in the Prosser home, would have no hesitation in piling on the back of her neck and whistling for stern-faced colleagues to come and fasten the gyves to her wrists. Better, then, that they should part. His going had deprived her of the pleasure of listening to his views on this and that and wondering how he could talk the way he did without having a potato in his mouth, but she had also lost the unpleasant feeling that centipedes were crawling up and down her spine which always affected her when hobnobbing with the gendarmerie.

It did not take her long to remove her wet dress and slip into the something loose represented by Freddie's pajamas, and she was on the whole in reasonably cheerful mood as she went down to the kitchen for the cup of hot coffee which she had mentioned. A certain chagrin was inevitable after she had come so near to success in the object of her quest and failed, owing to an act of God at the eleventh hour, to achieve her aims, but hers was a resilient and philosophical nature, and she was able to look on the bright side and count her blessings one by one. She was short, yes, of Prosser jewelry, and that, she would have been the first to admit, was in the nature of a sock in the eye, but she had at least the consoling thought that she had made a clean getaway when for an instant all had seemed lost.

She did not, however, look forward to telling Soapy of this third expeditionary disaster. He would sympathize, he would be all that a loving and understanding husband should be, but he would not be able to conceal that this was a blow. "Where do we go from here?" he would ask, and her only answer would be that she was goshdarned if she knew. It seemed to her, as it would seem to him, that every stone had been turned and every avenue explored. She could not keep on getting bright ideas indefinitely, and Soapy, except when he was selling oil stock, never had any.

It was as she mused thus, sipping coffee and thinking hard thoughts of Myrtle Prosser, whom it would have been a genuine pleasure to her to dip, feet first, into a vat of molten lead, that Freddie, alighting from the 6:03 down train, arriving Valley Fields 6:24, started to walk to Peacehaven.

The rain had stopped, which was all to the good, for he had gone out that morning without his umbrella, and not even the thought that, George being away for the evening, he would have to cook dinner for himself was able to affect his mood of *bien être*. Sally loved him, and he would shortly have a cool ten thousand pounds in his hip pocket, and, as for dinner, there were always sardines. As he latch-keyed himself into Peacehaven, one would not be far wrong in saying that there was a song on his lips.

There was also, it was borne in upon him as he entered, a song on somebody else's lips, the somebody in question apparently being in the kitchen, for as he parked hat on hatstand he could hear a distinct rendition of a popular ballad proceeding from that direction. This struck him as odd, for he had supposed that his cousin George, wafted Londonward on the wings of love, would have left long ere this. Another aspect of the matter that puzzled him was why George's voice, normally a pleasant baritone, should suddenly have become a highish soprano.

The singing ceased. Dolly had been doing it merely to cheer herself up, and this object she had now succeeded in accomplishing. She finished washing her coffee cup and the knife with which she had cut herself a slice of seed cake, and came into the living room, giving Freddie much the same feeling of having had a bomb touched off under him as the ghost of Banquo on a memorable occasion gave Macbeth. In the days before his roving affections had centered on Sally he had had a good deal of experience of girls popping up at unexpected moments in unexpected places, but he had never seen one before wearing his pajamas. A perfect stranger, too, it seemed to him—which deepened the bizarre note.

Then Dolly, who felt that it was for her to open the conversation, said, "Hi, brother Widgeon! How's tricks?" and he recognized her as the wife of Mr. Molloy, his benefactor. He was conscious of a passing wish that this woman would not keep flitting into his life every hour on the hour like a family specter, but she was linked by marriage to the man who had set his feet on the ladder of affluence by letting him have that Silver River stock, so she must not be allowed to think that her presence was unwelcome.

Replacing his heart, which had bumped against his front teeth, he said, "Oh, hullo, there you are."

"Nice meeting you again."

"Nice of you to drop in. Beastly weather, what?"

"You said it."

"Seems to be clearing up a bit, though, now."

"That's good."

"Rain's stopped."

"Probably just biding its time."

"I shouldn't wonder. Care for a cup of tea?"

"I've had some coffee."

"Have some more."

"No, thanks. Well, I guess I ought to explain why I've butted in this way."

"Not at all. Any time you're passing."

"That's just what I was doing—passing. And that storm suddenly came on, and I was getting soaked, so I dashed in here."

"I get the idea. For shelter, as it were?"

"That's right. Nobody can say I haven't sense enough to come in out of the rain, ha, ha."

"Ha, ha," echoed Freddie, but not blithely. Once again he was thinking of what Sally would make of all this, were it to be drawn to her attention.

"I borrowed your pajamas on account of if I stuck around in a wet dress, I might get a cold."

"Or pneumonia. Quite right."

"You aren't sore?"

"No, no."

"I wish I could say the same of myself. Coming here in such a rush, I fell and scraped my knee, and it's kind of acting up."

"Good heavens!"

"Rubbed quite a bit of skin off it. Take a look."

"At your knee?"

"That's the knee I mean."

A wrinkle creased the smoothness of Freddie's brow. His devotion to Sally being one hundred per cent, if not more, it was wholly foreign to his policy to take a look at the knees of others of her sex, especially of those so spectacularly comely as Mrs. Thomas G. Molloy. A year ago he would have sprung to the task, full of the party spirit, but now he was a changed, deeper man who had put all that sort of thing behind him. However, he was also a host, and a host cannot indulge his personal feelings.

"Right ho," he said. "Let's have a dekko. Egad," he went on, having had it, "that doesn't look too good. You ought to see the tribal medicine man about it. Nasty flesh wound, might cause lockjaw. And you don't want that."

Dolly admitted that she had no great fondness for lockjaw.

"The only catch is that you can't very well go charging about Valley Fields, looking for doctors, in striped pajamas. I'll tell you what," said Freddie. "My cousin George has some iodine. I'll go and fetch it."

"Too bad, giving you all this trouble."

"No trouble, no trouble at all. And George won't mind. You haven't met him, have you?"

"Why, yes, I did run into him for a moment."

"Nice chap."

"Yeah. Not like most cops I know."

"Do you know a lot of cops?"

"Well, not socially, but I've seen them around. Over in the States they're kind of tough."

"I know what you mean. Not bonhomous."

"They don't know how to treat a lady, the flat-footed sons of bachelors."

"I'll bet they don't. Well, ho for the iodine. George keeps it in his room."

The window of George's room looked on the back garden, and if Freddie had happened to glance out of it, he would have observed a slim figure making its way to the back door of Castlewood. Sally—for, as Leila Yorke was fond of saying in her novels, it was she—had no latchkey and did not want to disturb her employer by ringing the front doorbell.

She entered the rear premises and reaching the living room found Leila Yorke reading a magazine.

"Sorry I couldn't get back earlier," she said. "Busy day. How did the interview go off?"

"Better than I had expected," said Leila Yorke. "Most interviewers in my experience are recruited from homes for the mentally afflicted, but this one was a nice bright girl. We got along like anything. But a curious thing happened. She suddenly disappeared."

"Faded away, you mean, like the Cheshire Cat?"

"As far as I can make out, she must have gone into the garden and left that way."

"In all that rain? Odd."

"That's what I thought, but I wasn't giving it much attention, as I was coping at the time with Mrs. Prosser."

"Oh, did she come? Freddie's friend Oofy's wife? To reason with you about the book, I suppose?"

"Yes, she talked for hours and would be talking still, if I hadn't edged her to the door and pushed her out. But I don't want to sit chewing the fat about Ma Prosser. Tell me what happened when you saw Johnnie Shoesmith."

"Well, I went in."

"Yes?"

"And he gave me a nasty look."

"Was that all?"

"No, he gave me several more in the course of our chat. Would you call him a very genial sort of man?"

"Johnnie can be the world's leading louse when he likes, and he seems to like all the time these days. Comes of being a solicitor. They get soured. Did he recommend a private eye?"

"Yes, I suppose you could call it that. He grabbed the telephone directory, looked at the classified section and picked the name at the top of the list, a man called Adair, J. Sheringham Adair."

"Nonsense. There isn't such a name."

"Well, that's what he says it is. I went to see him, and there it was in large letters on his door. He's got a dingy little office in a dingy little backwater called Halsey Court. It's in Mayfair, so I suppose he thinks of himself as a Mayfair consultant."

"What's he like?"

"A frightful little man with a face like a monkey and a waxed mustache."

"Is he any good, do you think?"

"He said he was. He spoke most highly of himself."

"I imagine all these private eyes are much alike. Oh, well, let's hope for the best."

"That's the way to talk. He's coming here to see you and get a photograph of your husband. Can you spare him one?"

"Dozens."

"Then, as you say, we'll hope for the best. And now, will you be wanting me for half an hour or so?"

"No. Why? Want to go to Peacehaven and see your Freddie?"

"That's the idea," said Sally. "Give him a nice surprise."

16.

Dolly's premonition that her tale of failure would remove the sunshine from Soapy's life and cause him to feel that it was hopeless to struggle further was amply fulfilled. Melancholy marked him for its own not only over the pre-dinner cocktails but at the meal that followed them and at next day's breakfast. A student of the classics, watching him eat eggs and bacon, would have been reminded of Socrates drinking the hemlock, and though it meant a lonely morning for her, she experienced a sense of relief when he exchanged his bedroom slippers for a pair of serviceable shoes and announced that he was going to take a walk and think things over. She found the spectacle of his drawn face painful.

It was a considerable time before he returned, and when he did she was amazed to observe that his face, so far from being drawn, was split toward the middle by a smile so dazzling that she blinked at the sight of it. His opening remark, that everything was now as smooth as silk and that they were sitting pretty, deepened her bewilderment. She loved him dearly and yielded to no one in her respect for his ability to sell worthless oil stock to the least promising of prospects, but, except for this one great gift of his, she had no illusions about his intelligence. She knew that she had taken for better or worse one who was practically the twin brother of Mortimer Snerd, and she liked it. It was her view that brains only unsettle a husband, and she was comfortably conscious of herself possessing enough for the two of them.

"Sitting pretty?" she gasped. It seemed incredible to her that the briskest of walks could have given her loved one anything even remotely resembling an idea. "How do you figure that out?"

Soapy sank into a chair and took off his left shoe.

"Got a blister," he announced.

It was no time for wifely sympathy. When pain and anguish wring the left foot, a woman ought, of course, to be a ministering angel, but Dolly's impatience temporarily unfitted her for the role.

"How do you mean, we're sitting pretty?"

"Rustle up the lifesavers, and I'll tell you. The thing's in the bag."

Dolly rustled up the lifesavers, and he became even brighter at the sight of them.

"Gee!" he said, regarding her fondly between sips. "You look like a new red wagon, baby."

"Never mind how I look," said Dolly, though pleased by the compliment. "What's happened?"

"You mean the blister? It came on when I'd been walking about half an hour," said Soapy, massaging his foot, "and I felt as if I had a red-hot coal in my shoe. You ever had a blister?"

A dangerous look crept into Dolly's face.

"Get on," she said. "Tell me in a few simple words what's given you this idea that we're sitting pretty?"

She spoke quietly, but Soapy had been married long enough to know that a wife's quiet tones are best respected. He embarked on his narrative without further preamble.

"Well, sir, just after I got this blister, who do you think I met? Chimp."

Dolly sniffed. As has been stated, Chimp Twist was no favorite of hers. Circumstances in the past had sometimes led to their being associated in business deals, but he ranked in her affections even lower than Mrs. Alexander Prosser.

"Must just have made your day, seeing that little weasel," she said acidly, and Soapy's smile became broader.

"It did," he said, "because what do you think he told me?"

"If it was the time, I'll bet he lied about it."

"He told me Leila Yorke has engaged him to find her husband."

"Has she one?"

"Seems so, by all accounts, and she's hired Chimp to locate him."

"He's disappeared?"

"That's what he's done, and Chimp's got the job of looking for him."

"So what?"

Soapy's eyes widened in surprise. He had supposed his mate to be quicker at the uptake than this.

"So *what?*" he said. "Use your bean, baby. Why, can't you see, there he'll be, in and out of the house, having conferences and what not all the time, and don't tell me he won't find a chance sooner or later of getting up to that room and putting his hooks on the ice."

"But he doesn't know it's there."

"Sure he knows. I told him."

"What!"

A strong shudder had shaken Dolly from the top of her perm to the alligator shoes for which a leading department store had been looking everywhere since she had last paid them a visit. Her eyes bulged and her lips parted as if she were about to reveal to her mate just what she thought of this last stupendous act of folly. She did not do this because she loved him and knew that it was his misfortune rather than his fault that he was solid bone from the neck up, but the gasping cry she uttered was enough to make it clear to him that all was not well.

"You *told* him?"

Soapy was perplexed. His story was not going as well as he had expected.

"Well, I had to, baby, or he wouldn't have known where to look."

Again, Dolly's lips parted, and again she closed them. It is possible that she was counting ten, that infallible specific against reckless speech.

"He's going to see her this afternoon, he says. Why, for all we know, he might come back with that ice this evening. Beats me why you don't seem pleased, baby. Here we were, all washed up with no chance of getting the stuff, and along comes this wonderful bit of luck that solves everything. It isn't as if Chimp wants the earth. He said he would do it for ten per cent of the gross."

"And you believed him?"

"Sure I believed him. Why wouldn't I?"

"Because you know as well as I do that Chimp Twist is as crooked as a pretzel. What he hasn't learned about double-crossing you could write on a postage stamp. Shall I tell you what's going to happen, in case you're interested? Reach me down my crystal ball for a moment, and I'll peer into the future and give you the dope. Ha! The mists clear, and I see a little rat with a waxed mustache and a face that only a mother could love hurrying down to Valley Fields. He goes into Castlewood. He's sneaking up the stairs to the bedroom. He's looking on top of the wardrobe. What's that he's putting in his pocket? A bag of peanuts? No, by golly, it's the ice I got from Mrs. Prosser. You remember that ice? I was telling you about it the other day. And now what do I behold? Can he be heading for the nearest airport? Yeah, that's what he's doing. Now they're telling him to fasten his safety belt. Now the winged monster soars above the clouds, and unless it falls and he breaks his damn neck his next address'll be Box 243, rural free delivery, somewhere in South America. And who are these two poor slobs I can see, sitting watching and waiting and saying, 'Ain't he ever coming?' Their faces seem familiar somehow. Why, it's you and me! Yessir, that's who it is, it's us!"

Dolly paused, panting a little, and Soapy's lower jaw fell slowly like a tired flower drooping on its stem. He was not as a rule an easy man to explain things to, but on this occasion his wife's reasoning had been too lucid to allow of any misunderstanding. He had got the message.

"I never thought of that," he said.

"Give a mite of attention to it now."

"Gee!"

"Gee is right."

"What are we going to do if he hijacks the stuff?"

"Sue him," said Dolly, and even Soapy could discern that she spoke satirically. He fell into what would have been a thoughtful silence, if he had been capable of thinking. The best he was able to suggest at the end of several minutes was that he should telephone Leila Yorke and warn her to have nothing to do with J. Sheringham Adair, whose private-eye activities were a mere cloak or front for criminality of the lowest order.

"So then, if he comes trying to ooze into the house, she'll go into action with that gun of hers."

Dolly was not impressed.

"You think she'll have a lot of confidence in what you tell her, after that session you had with her about Silver River Oil and Refinery?"

"I could say I was Inspector Somebody speaking from Scotland Yard."

"With a Middle Western accent? Try again."

Soapy had finished his martini, but though agreeable to the taste and imparting a gentle glow, it brought no inspiration. He chewed his lip, and said it was difficult, and Dolly said Yeah, she had noticed that herself.

Soapy scratched his Shakespearean forehead.

"I don't know what to suggest."

"Make that double."

"We might . . . No, that's no good. Or . . . No, that's no good, either."

"Not so hot as your first idea. That first one seemed to me to have possibilities."

"If only," said Soapy wistfully, "there was some way of getting that dame out of the house!"

Dolly, who like a good wife had been refilling his glass,

paused with the shaker in mid-air, spellbound. She had not expected to hear so keen a summing-up of the situation from such a source. Out of the mouths of babes and sucklings, she seemed to be saying to herself.

"Get her out of the house? Soapy, I believe you've got something. When I was down there yesterday, she sort of gave me the impression that it wouldn't take a lot to make her pack up and leave. I got the idea she's kind of pining for that stately home of hers, where there's cooks and butlers and all like that. Nothing she actually said, but that's the way it struck me. Look, finish that up and go take a walk around the block."

"What, with this blister of mine?"

"Well, keep quiet, then. I want to think," said Dolly, and she walked to the window and stood looking out on London, while Soapy, scarcely daring to breathe lest he destroy thought at its source, lay back in his chair and gently massaged the sole of his left foot, his gaze fixed on her occipital bone as intently as if he could see the brain working behind it. The light of hope in his eyes was only faint, but it was there. Not once but many times in the past had his wife's little gray cells brought triumph out of disaster, and it might be that even the current problem, which, he freely admitted, was a lalapalooza, would not prove too much for her.

At length, Dolly spoke. "Soapy, come here. I want to show you something."

Soapy came as directed, and he too looked out on London. The portion of it that he saw was the back premises of Barribault's Hotel, for it was in that direction that the window faced. It was not a very exhilarating spectacle, mostly empty boxes and ash cans, and it did little to lighten the gloom in which he was plunged. Not that he would have derived any greater spiritual refreshment from it if the boxes had been the Champs Élysées in springtime and the ash cans the Taj Mahal by moonlight.

"See that cat?" said Dolly.

The cat to which she alluded was an animal of raffish and bohemian aspect, the sort of cat that hangs around street corners and makes low jokes to other cats as anti-social as itself. It was nosing about in the ash cans below, and Soapy regarded it without enthusiasm. He was not, he said, fond of cats.

"Nor's the Yorke dame," said Dolly. "One came into the garden while I was there and started stalking a bird, and she eased it out."

"With her shotgun?"

"No, she just hollered, and the cat streaked off, and then she told me she didn't like cats."

"And so?"

"Seeing that one down there gave me the idea."

Soapy was stirred to his depths.

"You haven't got an idea?" he said reverently.

"I have, too. Wait. Don't talk," said Dolly. She went to the ornate writing table with which all suites at Barri-bault's Hotel are provided and took pen and paper, frown-ing meditatively.

"How do you spell 'descriptions'?" she asked. "No, it's okay. I know."

"*D* as in *doughnut—*"

"All right, all *right*. I tell you I know. Is Castlewood *t-l-e* or *t-e-l*?"

"*T-l-e*. Why, honey? What is all this?"

Dolly waved him down impatiently, as authors will when interrupted with questions in the middle of an im-portant work, and for some moments concentrated tensely on whatever this literary composition of hers was, her fore-head wrinkled and the tip of her tongue protruding a little. After what seemed an hour she rose and handed him a sheet of notepaper.

"How's this?" she said.

It was not a lengthy document. It read:

WANTED

CATS OF ALL DESCRIPTIONS

GOOD PRICES PAID

APPLY

CASTLEWOOD

MULBERRY GROVE

VALLEY FIELDS.

"It'll cost money," said Dolly, "on account of it's got to go in all the papers including the local ones down Valley Fields way. I know there's one called the *South London Argus* and there may be half a dozen more. That's up to you to find out. I want them in tomorrow morning, so you'll have to do some getting around, even if you do have a blister. But it'll bring home the bacon, believe me."

Soapy was examining the script with the puzzled eye of one who is not abreast.

"How do you mean, bring home the bacon, baby?"

"That's the way I figure it. I told you the Yorke dame wasn't any too strong for Valley Fields anyway, so what happens when hundreds of people come horning in on her with cats of all descriptions and prob'ly letting half of them loose in the garden? And if the cats don't do the trick, we can switch to something else. There's plenty of other things. I say she'll pack up and leave pronto. Am I right, or am I right?"

Soapy drew a long breath. Even to him all things had been made clear, and he was telling himself that he had known all along that the light of his life would find a way.

"Baby," he said, when emotion allowed him to speak, "there's no one—"

"Say, tell you something," said Dolly happily. "I'm beginning to think that myself."

17.

Tucked away in odd corners of the aristocratic Mayfair section of London there exist, like poor relations of the rich, certain alleys and byways which would be far more at home in the humbler surroundings of Whitechapel or Shoreditch. Halsey Court was one of these. Leila Yorke, on her way to the offices of the J. Sheringham Adair investigation agency two mornings after Dolly had put her plan of campaign into action, found it dark, dirty, dismal and depressing, and far too full of prowling cats. Circumstances had so arranged themselves on the previous day as to make her reluctant, if she lived to be a hundred, ever to see another cat again.

She mounted the three flights of stone stairs that led to

the dingy room where Chimp Twist passed his days and, with a brief nod, dusted a chair and sat down, eying him with the intentness of a woman who had come for professional advice and meant to get it.

He was not a very exhilarating spectacle. Sally, drawing a word picture of him for her benefit, had called him a frightful little man with a face like a monkey and a waxed mustache, and when he had come to Castlewood to obtain a photograph of her husband Leila Yorke had been struck by the accuracy of the description. But one does not engage an investigator for his looks. What counts is brain, and she had been favorably impressed by his obvious sagacity. Like Dolly, she would not have trusted him to tell her the right time, but she was not proposing to trust him. All she wanted from him was his trained assistance in tracking down the unknown hellhound responsible for the quite untrue statement that she was in need of cats of all descriptions.

"Hope I'm not interrupting you when you're busy on the mysterious affair of the maharajah's ruby," she said, "but I'd like a conference."

Chimp leaned back and put the tips of his fingers together.

"With reference to the matter we were discussing when I visited your residence, madam?" he said, assuming the manner and diction he always employed with clients. In private life he spoke in the vernacular and generally out of the side of his mouth, but in his official capacity he modeled his style on the more gentlemanly detectives in the books he read. "I can assure you that everything is being done to bring that to a successful conclusion. My whole organization is working on it. Half a dozen of my best men are busy on the investigation at this moment. Let me see, who did I put on the case? Wilbraham, Jones,

Evans, Meredith, Schwed—yes, fully half a dozen. They are scouring London from end to end. It is as if you had pressed a button and set in motion some vast machine. The Adair agency is like a kind of octopus, stretching its tentacles hither and thither and—"

Leila Yorke was not a patient woman. She banged the desk, causing a cloud of dust to rise, and Chimp's voice trailed away. Better men than he had fallen silent when Leila Yorke banged desks—Aubrey Popgood of her firm of publishers for one and Cyril Grooly, his partner, for another, and similar effects had been produced on headwaiters in restaurants when she banged tables. As she sometimes explained to intimate friends, it was all in the follow-through.

"In short," she said, "you're telling me you're good."

Chimp admitted that this was what he had intended to convey.

"Right," said Leila Yorke briskly. "So now we've settled that, perhaps you will let me mention what I've come about."

"*Not* the matter we were discussing when I visited your residence?"

"No. Cats."

Chimp blinked. "Did you say cats?"

"And dogs."

"I don't think I quite follow you, madam."

"You will," said Leila Yorke, and opening her bag she produced a wad of newspaper clippings. "Read those."

Chimp put on a pair of horn-rimmed spectacles. Seeing him in his normal state, one would have said that nothing could make him look more repulsive, but these glasses went far toward performing that miracle. Even Leila Yorke, though a strong woman, winced at the sight. He read the clippings and raised a surprised and inquiring eye.

"You are fond of cats, madam?"

"I like them in moderation, always provided they don't go for the birds, but you don't suppose I put those advertisements in the papers, do you? Somebody's playing a practical joke on me, and I want you to find out who it is, so that I can strangle him with my bare hands. Cats of all descriptions! I'll say they were. I don't know how many people there are living in South London, but they all called at Castlewood yesterday, and every damned one of them was carrying a blasted cat and wanted me either to buy it or pay him for the time I'd wasted telling him to bring it. I never saw so many cats in my life. I was up to my waist in them. Black cats, tabby cats, striped cats, cats with bits chewed out of their ears—it was like a mouse's nightmare. And more coming every minute. If it hadn't been for Widgeon's cousin George, they'd have been there still."

She paused, her eyes gleaming as she relived those testing moments, and Chimp asked who Widgeon's cousin George was.

"He's a policeman. He and Widgeon have got the house next door. He suddenly appeared and told the multitude to pass along, which they did, and I don't blame them. I'd have passed along myself if a man that size had told me to. Thank heaven for policemen, I say. Salt of the earth, those boys."

Chimp preserved a rather prim silence. He did not share her enthusiasm for the constabulary, with whom his relations both in his native country and in England had been far from cordial. Fewer and less vigilant officers were what both the United States and Great Britain needed, in his opinion, if they were to have any chance of becoming earthly Paradises.

"Very efficient, that Cousin George. Got lots of weight, and threw it about like a hero. I suppose he was grateful to me because I'd taken two of the five-shilling tickets for the concert in aid of the Policemen's Orphanage. Just shows it was right what the fellow said about casting your bread on the waters. He couldn't have been more zealous if I'd bought up the entire front row of orchestra stalls. Well, that ended the episode of the cats."

Chimp said that was satisfactory, and Leila Yorke corrected him.

"Not so darned satisfactory, because this morning there were the dogs, and he wasn't around to cope with them."

"Dogs, madam?"

"How many breeds of dogs are there?"

Chimp was unable to supply the information, but said he thought there were a good many.

"Well, representatives of every known breed were there this morning with the exception of Mexican Chihuahuas. I don't think I noticed any of them among those present, though I may be wrong. I'm fond of dogs, mind you, I've got six of them at home in the country, but—"

"Castlewood is not your home?"

"No, I only took the place because I was planning to write a book about the suburbs. I live at Loose Chippings in Sussex, and I'm beginning to wish I was back there. A little more of this, and Valley Fields will have seen the last of me. What's the matter?"

What had prompted the questions had been a sudden aguelike quiver which had run through her companion's weedy frame, causing his waxed mustache to behave like a tuning fork. Chimp Twist was, as has been indicated, astute, and a blinding light had flashed upon him. As clearly as if she had appeared before him and given him the low-down herself, he saw behind these unusual occurrences the shapely hand of Mrs. Thomas G. Molloy. His client had spoken of practical jokers. There was nothing of the practical joker about Dolly Molloy. She was strictly a businesswoman, actuated always by business motives. And Soapy, the dumb brick, had told him all about that ice, even to the very spot where it was hidden. It figured, he was saying to himself; yes, it certainly figured.

He stilled his vibrating mustache with a quick hand, and leaned forward—impressively, he hoped, though actually the impression he gave Leila Yorke was that he was about to have some sort of fit.

"Has it occurred to you, madam, that the person who inserted these advertisements may have been trying to force you to leave Castlewood because there is something there he wants to secure and will be able to secure if the house becomes unoccupied?"

Leila Yorke considered the suggestion, and after the briefest of moments placed it in the class of those she did not think much of. No doubt England's criminals included in their ranks a certain number of eccentrics, but she refused to believe that even these would go to so much trouble to obtain an aspidistra, a reproduction of Millais's "Huguenot" and a china mug with "A Present from Bognor Regis" on it in pink sea shells.

"What on earth is there in Castlewood for anyone to want?" she demanded.

"Possibly the object is buried in the garden."

"Not a bone, or those dogs would have got it."

Chimp's expression, though not losing the respectfulness due to a client, showed that he deplored this frivolity.

His manner became more portentous, his diction more orotund.

"If I am right in supposing that there is something of value concealed on the premises, it is to be presumed that it was placed there by some recent occupant of the house. It would be interesting to find out who was the tenant of Castlewood before you."

"I know that. Cornelius told me. It was someone called Molloy."

Chimp started dramatically. "Molloy?"

"So Cornelius said."

"An American?"

"Yes."

"A large man with a high forehead?"

"I don't know. I never saw him," said Leila Yorke, unaware that she had had that pleasure and privilege. "Why?"

"I am wondering if it can have been a dangerous crook known as Soapy Molloy. Who, by the way, is Cornelius?"

"The house agent."

"With your permission I will call him up. This cannot be a mere coincidence," said Chimp, rummaging in a drawer for the telephone book. "The name Molloy, and all these strange, one might say sinister, happenings. Suspicious, very suspicious. Mr. Cornelius?" he said. "This is the J. Sheringham Adair detective agency. We have been asked by Scotland Yard to assist them with some questions regarding a man named Molloy, who occupied a house called Castlewood until recently. Scotland Yard thinks this may be the same Molloy in whom they are interested. Could you describe him to me? . . . I see . . . Yes . . . yes . . . thank you." He hung up, and turned to Leila Yorke with an air of quiet triumph. "It is the same man, not a doubt of it."

"But who is he?" asked Leila Yorke, impressed. There

had been a period since she entered this office when its dustiness and dinginess had shaken her faith in its proprietor, but it was now quite solid again. What is a little dust, she was feeling, if the head it settles on contains a keen, incisive brain?

Chimp fondled his mustache.

"Soapy Molloy, though nothing has as yet been proved against him, nothing that would stand up in court, is known to be the head of an international drug ring which the police have been trying to smash for years, and I think we may take it as certain that he has buried a large consignment of the dope in the garden of Castlewood. No other explanation seems to meet the case. You must leave the house immediately, madam."

Leila Yorke's jaw tightened, and her blue eyes glowed with an offended light.

"What, let myself be chased out of my home by a blasted dope peddler?"

Chimp hastened to soothe her wounded pride.

"It is merely a ruse. Thinking the house is unoccupied, Molloy will act. But it will not be unoccupied. I shall be there."

"You?"

"What I suggest is this. You return to your home in Sussex tonight and tell this Mr. Cornelius that you are leaving. Molloy is certain to get in touch with him tomorrow or the day after to find out if his efforts to get rid of you have been successful. He will come to Castlewood, thinking the coast is clear, and I shall be waiting for him."

"You'd better borrow my shotgun."

"Unnecessary. I shall have some of my best men with me—Meredith certainly and possibly Schwed. Three of us will be enough to overpower this scoundrel."

"I thought Meredith and Schwed were looking for my husband."

"I shall take them off the case, but only for a few hours. I am expecting Molloy to make his move tomorrow night. We must oblige Scotland Yard."

"Why? I'm not worrying about Scotland Yard's troubles. I want to find Joe."

"We shall find him, madam. The Sheringham Adair Agency never fails. You will leave Castlewood tonight?"

"I suppose so, if you say so."

"Then that is settled. You will telephone me directly you are leaving?"

"Very well."

"And what did you say your address in the country was?"

"Claines Hall, Loose Chippings."

"I'll send my bill to you there," said Chimp, and having ushered his client to the door with a suavity of which those who knew him best would never have thought him capable, opened another drawer of the desk and produced the bottle of whisky without which, as is generally known, no detective agency can function. As he drank, a glow suffused him, due partly to the generous strength of the spirit but even more to the thought that he was about to slip a quick one over on the Mrs. Thomas G. Molloy who in the past had so often slipped quick ones over on him.

Leila Yorke, meanwhile, had groped her way out of the twilight dimness of Halsey Court and wandered into Bond Street to do a little window-shopping before lunch. She was thus enabled to encounter Freddie Widgeon, who was on his way to enjoy, if it could be called enjoying, the hospitality of his uncle Lord Blicester. An invitation, equivalent to a royal command, had reached him on the previous day.

Leila Yorke was delighted to see Freddie. She had been contemplating a solitary meal, and she disliked solitary meals.

"Hullo there, Widgeon," she said. "The hour has produced just the man I wanted."

Her interview with Chimp Twist had left her in excellent spirits. The prospect of getting away from Valley Fields, shocking as this would have seemed to Mr. Cornelius, elated her. She wanted to be back at Claines Hall, Loose Chippings, at her familiar desk, writing the same old tripe she had always written, and no more of this nonsense of being stark and gray and significant. It amazed her that she had ever dreamed of trying to top that gloomy historian of the suburbs, the late George Gissing. Even as she gazed into the jeweler's window, there had come into her head the germ of an idea for a story about a man named Claude and a girl called Jessamine who had gray eyes and hair the color of ripe wheat.

"Oh, hullo," said Freddie. He seemed to her distrait and out of tune with her joyous mood. "How have you been lately? Bobbing along? My cousin George tells me you've been having cat trouble."

"A spot," said Leila Yorke buoyantly, "the merest spot. I'll tell you all about it while you're giving me lunch."

"Frightfully sorry, but I can't give you lunch. I'm fixed up with my Uncle Rodney."

"Where?"

"Barribault's."

"I'll join you," said Leila Yorke.

18.

Catering as it does mainly to Texas millionaires who have just learned that another oil well has been discovered on their property and maharajahs glad to have got away from the pomp and ceremony of the old palace for a while, there is always an atmosphere of hearty—though never unrefined —gaiety about the lobby of Barribault's Hotel at the luncheon hour, and it was an atmosphere that fitted well with Leila Yorke's mood. Freed from the cloying society of the Castlewood cats and stimulated by her recent interview with J. Sheringham Adair, she had recovered all her normal exuberance. The dullest eye could discern that she was in the pink. Far too much so, Freddie considered, as he eyed her morosely. Wanting to be alone to brood on his grief, preferably in some cemetery, he found her vivacity hard to bear.

"Widgeon," she said, raising her glass and beaming with good will, "I would like you to join me in a toast, and no heeltaps. To the fellow who first invented life, for he started a darned good thing. What did you say?"

Freddie, who had said "Oh?" said he had said "Oh?" and she proceeded.

"You see before you, Widgeon, a woman who, if such goings-on were allowed in this posh caravanserai, would be clapping her hands in glee and dancing around on the tips of her toes."

"Oh?" said Freddie.

"Today, and you may give this to the press, I am glad, glad, glad, like Pollyanna, and with good reason. I have seen the light and realize what a mug's game it was ever to think of writing that stark novel of squalor I spoke to you about. I have abandoned the idea in toto."

"Oh?" said Freddie.

"There rose before me the vision of all those thousands of half-witted women waiting with their tongues out for their next ration of predigested pap from my pen, and I felt it would be cruel to disappoint them. Be humane, I told myself. Who am I to deprive them of their simple pleasures, I soliloquized. Keep faith with your public, my girl, I added, still soliloquizing."

"Oh?" said Freddie.

"And there was another aspect of the matter. Inasmuch as these blighted novels of squalor have to be at least six hundred pages long, hammering one out would have been the most ghastly sweat, and the first lesson an author must learn is how to make things as easy for himself as possible. The ideal toward which one strives is unconscious cerebration. I look forward to a not distant date when I shall be able to turn out the stuff in my sleep."

"Oh?" said Freddie.

She gave him a sharp glance. Though preferring always to bear the major burden of any conversation in which she took part, she liked more give-and-take than this. A little one-sided this exchange of ideas was becoming, she felt.

"Aren't you saying 'Oh?' a good deal as of even date?" she said. "You seem distrait, Widgeon."

"I am a bit."

"What's eating you?"

Freddie laughed a mirthless laugh, the sort of laugh a lost soul in an inferno might have uttered, if tickled by some observation on the part of another lost soul.

"What isn't?"

"Hard morning at the office?"

"Well, I got fired, if you call that hard."

Leila Yorke was all warmhearted sympathy.

"My poor unhappy boy! What was the trouble?"

"Oh, nothing you'd understand. Technical stuff. I made a bloomer yesterday when copying out an affidavit, as the foul things are called, and when I arrived this morning—late again, because I'd been hanging round trying to get a word with Sally—Shoesmith sent for me and applied the boot. He said he had felt the urge for a long time and had struggled to fight against it, but this had made it irresistible. He gave me a month's salary in lieu of notice, saying it was well worth the money to get rid of me immediately. He added that this was the happiest day of his life."

"Didn't you plead with him?"

"Certainly not. I ticked him off. Remembering what you had told me about his murky past, I said that I might not be his dream employee, but at least I didn't kiss girls behind rhododendron bushes. Oddly enough, I never have. Rose bushes, yes, but not rhododendrons. 'Kiss fewer girls behind rhododendron bushes, Shoesmith,' I said, and I turned on my heel and walked out."

"Very upsetting, I don't wonder you're feeling off your oats."

"Oh, it isn't that. Being fired doesn't worry me, because pretty soon I shall be making a vast fortune."

"How's that?"

"Sorry, I can't tell you," said Freddie, remembering Mr. Molloy's injunctions of secrecy. "It's just an investment of sorts I'm going to clean up on. No, what I'm down among the wines and spirits about," he went on, abandoning reserve in his desire to unburden himself to a sympathetic confidante, "is Sally. Has she told you what happened?"

"Not a word. What did happen?"

Freddie dipped his finger in his empty glass, secured the olive and swallowed it with a moody gulp.

"If something's gone wrong between you and Sally, you need another of those," said Leila Yorke maternally.

"You think so?"

"I'm sure of it. Waiter! Encore de martini cocktails. Talking of waiters," she said, as the man withdrew, "my missing husband's one."

"You don't say?"

"Saw him with my own eyes flitting to and fro with the hashed chicken in pastry at the Pen and Ink Club luncheon. But don't let's get off on the subject of my affairs. Everything's going to be all right as far as I'm concerned. I have an octopus stretching its tentacles hither and thither in search of him, and you know what these octopi are like. They never fail. Forget me and tell me about you and Sally. Have you really parted brass rags?"

"It looks like it."

"What did you do to the girl?"

"I didn't do anything."

"Come, come."

"It was my cousin George."

"The zealous officer who got into my ribs for ten of the best the other day for concert tickets? How does he come into it?"

Freddie scowled darkly at an inoffensive Texas millionaire who had seated himself at a nearby table. He had nothing specific against the man, but he was in the mood to scowl at anyone who came within his orbit of vision, and would have looked equally blackly at a visiting maharajah. When a Widgeon has lost the woman he loves, the general public is well advised to keep at a safe distance.

"I must begin by saying," he began by saying, "that of all the fatheaded, clothheaded half-wits that ever blew a police whistle, my cousin George is the worst. He's like that fellow in the poem whose name led all the rest."

"I know the fellow you mean. Had a spot of bother with angels getting into his bedroom in the small hours, if I remember rightly. So George is fatheaded, is he?"

"Has been from birth. But on this occasion he lowered all previous records. Oh, I know he has some sort of a story in . . . What's that word beginning with an x? It's on the tip of my tongue."

"Xylophone?"

"Extenuation. I know he can put up a kind of story in extenuation of his muttonheaded behavior. The woman was undoubtedly wet."

"You're going too fast for me. What woman?"

"This one who came to Peacehaven."

"Friend of yours?"

"I know her slightly."

"Ah!"

"Don't say 'Ah!' in that soupy tone of voice. Only the other day I had to rebuke Sally for doing the same thing. That, of course," said Freddie, heaving a sigh that seemed to come up from the soles of his shoes, "was when she and I were on speaking terms."

"Aren't you now?"

"Far from it. This morning I saw her in your garden and called to her, and she gave me the sort of look she would have given a leper she wasn't fond of and streaked back into the house. It was hanging round, hoping to establish contact again, that made me late at the office. Mark you, I can understand her point of view. She was unquestionably wearing my pajamas."

"Sally?"

"No, the woman."

"The one you know slightly?"

"Yes."

"Wearing your pajamas?"

"The ones with the purple stripe."

"H'm!"

Freddie raised a hand. Not even his cousin George, when on traffic duty, could have put more dignity into the gesture. On his face was a look rather similar to the one Sally had given him that morning in the garden.

"Don't say 'H'm!' It's as bad as 'Ah!' I could explain the whole thing so easily, if she'd only let me have a word with her and not shoot off like a sprinter hoping to break the hundred-yard record every time I open my mouth. This woman got caught in the rain and barged into Peacehaven for shelter. She met George, and he saw she was wet—"

"The trained eye! Nothing escapes the police."

"—and told her to go up to my room and get into my pajamas before she caught a nasty cold. He then went off to give his girl dinner, leaving her there, so when I got home, there I was, closeted with her."

"And Sally came in?"

"Not immediately. She entered at the moment when I was giving the woman a helping hand with her knee. She had fallen and scraped it, and I was putting iodine on it."

"On her knee?"

"Yes."

"Her *bare* knee?"

"Well, would she have been clad in sheet armor at such a moment?"

"H'm."

Freddie repeated the Georgelike gesture which had resulted from her previous use of this monosyllable.

"Will you *please* not say 'H'm!' The whole episode was pure to the last drop. Dash it, if a female has shaved about three inches of skin off her lower limbs and lockjaw is imminent unless prompt steps are taken through the proper channels, a fellow has to rally round with the iodine, hasn't he? You can't have women dying in awful agonies all over the sitting-room floor."

"Something in that. But Sally got the wrong angle?"

"She appeared to misunderstand the position of affairs completely. I didn't see her at first, because I was bending over the flesh wound with my back turned, but I heard a sort of gasping yip and looked round, and there she was, goggling at me as if shocked to the core. For an instant there was silence, broken only by the sound of a voice saying 'Ouch!'—iodine, stings like the dickens—and then Sally said, 'Oh, I beg your pardon. I thought you were alone,' and exited left center. And by the time I'd rallied from the shock and dashed after her, she was nowhere in sight. The whole thing's a pretty ghastly mess," said Freddie, and frowned blackly again, this time at a peer of the realm who, as peers of the realm so often did, had dropped in at Barribault's for a quick one before lunch and was sitting at a table across the room.

Leila Yorke was frowning, too, but the crease in her brow was a thoughtful crease. She was weighing the evidence and sifting it. A stern expression came into her face. She tapped Freddie on the arm.

"Widgeon, look me in the eye."

He looked her in the eye.

"And answer me one question. Do you intend to do right by our Nell, or are you regarding this innocent girl as the mere plaything of an idle hour, as Angela Fosdyke said to Bruce Tallentyre in my *Heather o' the Hills* when she found him kissing her sister Jasmine at the Hunt Ball. It would be interesting to know, for on your answer much depends."

Freddie, being sunk in one of Barribault's settees, than which none in London are squashier and more yielding to the frame, was unable to draw himself to his full height, but he gave her a cold, dignified look which made quite a good substitute for that maneuver. His voice, when he spoke, shook a little.

"Are you asking me if I love Sally?"

"I am."

"Of course I do. I love her madly."

"Satisfactory, as far as it goes. But one must bear in mind that you love every girl you meet."

"Where did you hear that?"

"Sally told me. I had it straight from the horse's mouth."

Freddie pounded the table passionately. Leila Yorke, a specialist at that sort of thing, liked his wrist work.

"Listen," he said, speaking thickly. "Sally's all wrong about that. She's judging me on past form, and there was a time, I admit, when I was a bit inclined to flit from flower to flower and sip, but I gave all that up when she came along. There's no one in the ruddy world for me but her. You know Cleopatra?"

"By name."

"And the Queen of Sheba?"

"Just to nod to."

"Well, lump them both together, and what have you got? Something I wouldn't cross the road for, if there was a chance of being with Sally. And you ask me if I love her. Tchah!"

"What did you say?"

"When?"

"On the cue, 'ask me if I love her.'"

"I said 'Tchah!' meaning to imply that the question is absurd, loony, incompetent, immaterial and irrelevant, as Shoesmith would say. Love her? Of course I love her. If not, why do you suppose I'm going steadily off my rocker because she won't speak to me and looks at me as if I were something more than usually revolting she had found under a flat stone?"

Leila Yorke nodded. His simple eloquence had convinced her.

"Widgeon, I believe your story. Many women wouldn't, for if ever there was a narrative that exuded fishiness at every pore, this is it. But I've always been a pushover for tales of love. Do you know what I'm going to do? I'm going to phone her and apprise her of the facts. I'll square you with her."

"You think you can?"

"Leave it to me."

"I absolutely can't tell you how grateful I am."

"Don't give it a thought."

"Do it now!"

"Not now. I want my lunch. And here comes our host,"

said Leila Yorke, as the portly form of Rodney, Lord Blicester, came through the swing door. "I wonder if he's heard about Johnnie Shoesmith easing you off the payroll."

Much of the light that had been illuminating Freddie's face faded away. The fact that he was in for a stormy interview with an uncle who on these occasions never minced his words had been temporarily erased from his mind.

"I expect so."

"Well, chin up. He can't eat you."

"He'll have a jolly good try," said Freddie. He had a momentary illusion that the spinal cord running down his back had been replaced by some sort of jellied substance.

19.

There are lunches which are rollicking from start to finish, with gay shafts of wit flickering to and fro like lightning flashes, and others where the going is on the sticky side and a sense of oppression seems to weigh the revelers down like a London fog. The one presided over by Lord Blicester at the restaurant of Barribault's Hotel fell into the second class.

It was in no festive mood that he had come to Barribault's Hotel. Calling on Mr. Shoesmith earlier in the morning to inquire how that income tax thing was working out and being informed by him that his nephew's services had been dispensed with, he had planned on meeting Freddie to speak his mind in no uncertain manner to that young blot on the London scene, and in the taxi on his way to the tryst he had been rehearsing and polishing his lines, substituting here a stronger adjective, there a more forceful noun. The discovery that what he had been looking forward to as a tête-à-tête was going to be a three-some gave him an unpleasant feeling of being about to burst. No one was more alive than he to what is done and what is not done, and in the matter of pounding the stuffing out of an errant nephew when there are ladies present the book of etiquette, he knew, was rigid.

Throughout the meal, accordingly, his obiter dicta were few and his demeanor that of a volcano biding its time. And as Freddie appeared to be in a sort of trance and Leila Yorke's conversation was confined for the most part to comments on his increased weight since she had seen him last, coupled with recommendations of dietary systems which could not fail to cut him down to size, the thing was not a great social success.

But even the weariest river winds somewhere safe to sea, and when after the serving of coffee his fair guest left the table, saying that she had a telephone call to make, he prepared to relieve what Shakespeare would have called his stuff'd bosom of its pent-up contents. Fixing his nephew with a baleful eye, he said, "Well, Frederick," and Freddie said, "Oh, hullo, Uncle Rodney," as if noticing for the first time that his relative was among those present. His thoughts had been with Leila Yorke at the telephone. Observing the bright, encouraging smile she had given him as she left, he knew she would pitch it strong, but would she pitch it strong enough to overcome Sally's sales resistance? So much hung on the answer to this question that he was understandably preoccupied.

Lord Blicester proceeded to arrest his attention. When moved, as he was now, he had an oratorical delivery not unlike that of a minor prophet of Old Testament days rebuking the sins of the people, and this he supplemented with appropriate gestures. The peer of the realm, who had finished his quick one and had come into the restaurant and was lunching at a table across the way, became immediately aware as he watched the drama with an interested eyeglass, that the thin feller over there was copping it properly from the fat feller, probably his uncle or something of that sort. His sympathies were with the thin feller. In his youth he, too, had known what it was to cop it from his elders. He belonged to a family whose senior members, when stirred, had never hesitated to dish it out.

It is one of the drawbacks to the historian's task that in recording dialogue between his characters he must select and abridge, giving merely the gist of their remarks and not a full stenographic transcript. It will be enough to say, therefore, that Lord Blicester, touching on his nephew's moral and spiritual defects, left nothing unspoken. The word "wastrel" occurred with some frequency, as did the adjective "hopeless." By the time he had rounded into his peroration, the conclusion anyone hearing it would have come to was that it was a mystery how such a despicable member of the human family as Frederick Fotheringay Widgeon had ever been allowed inside a respectable establishment like Barribault's Hotel.

The effect of this philippic on Freddie was to make him feel like somebody who had been caught in the San Francisco earthquake of 1906. He wilted visibly and was shrinking still further inside his well-cut flannel suit, when something occurred that stiffened his sinews, summoned up the blood and made him feel that it was about time he sat up and did a bit of talking back. Through the door of the restaurant two lunchers had entered and taken a table near the peer of the realm. One was Oofy Prosser, the other Soapy Molloy. They had been having an *apéritif* in Soapy's suite, and Oofy had just written out a check for a further block of Silver River stock, thanking Soapy with a good deal of effusiveness for letting him have it.

The sight of Soapy had an instant effect on Freddie's morale. The spate of injurious words proceeding from his uncle's lips had completely driven from his mind the thought that in a very short time he would be a rich man, on his way to Kenya to become still richer. It now came back to him, reminding him that there was absolutely no necessity for him to sit taking lip like this from an obese relation who, instead of saying offensive things to his nearest and dearest, would have been better employed having Turkish baths and going easy on the bread and potatoes.

He felt his calm, strong self again, and in the way he drew himself erect in his chair there was something suggestive of a worm coming out after a heavy thunderstorm. He knew himself to be more than equal to the task of telling a dozen two-hundred-and-fifty-pound uncles where they got off.

"That's all right, Uncle Rodney," he said briskly, "and there is possibly much in what you say, but, be that as it may, you don't know the half of it."

It would be erroneous to say that this defiant tone from one on whom he had been looking as less than the dust beneath his chariot wheels caused Lord Blicester to swell with indignation, for he had already swollen so far that a little more would have made him come apart at the seams. He had to content himself with glaring.

"I don't understand you."

"I'll make it clear to the meanest intelligence . . . That is . . . Well, you know what I mean. Let me begin by asking you something. You're all steamed up about Shoesmith taking the high road and me the low road and our relations being severed and all that, but how would you like being a sort of glorified office boy in a solicitor's firm?"

"The question does not arise."

"Yes, it does, because I've jolly well arisen it. The answer is that you wouldn't like it a bit. Nor do I. I want to go to Kenya and become a Coffee King."

"That nonsense again!"

"Not nonsense at all. Sound, practical move."

"You said you needed three thousand pounds to put into the business. You won't get it from me."

Freddie waved an airy hand. The peer of the realm, who was now eating *truite bleu,* paused in admiration with the fork at his lips. He had not thought the thin feller had it in him. Something seemed to have bucked the thin feller up, and good luck to him, felt the peer of the realm. He had just recognized Lord Blicester as a member of one of his clubs whose method of eating soup he disliked, and he was all for it if the thin feller was going to put him in his place.

"Keep your gold, Uncle Rodney," said Freddie, wishing too late that he had made it "dross." "I don't want it. I'm rolling in the stuff."

"What!"

"Literally rolling. Or shall be shortly. Turn the old loaf about ten degrees to the nor'-nor'east. See that bimbo at that table over there? Not the one with the pimples, the other one. Rich American financier."

Lord Blicester looked behind him.

"Why, it's Molloy!"

Freddie was surprised.

"You know him?"

"Certainly. He controls a stock in which I am interested."

"What's it called?"

"I fail to see what concern it is of yours, but its name is Silver River Oil and Refinery."

"Good Lord! You've got some of that?"

"I have."

"So have I."

Lord Blicester stared.

"You?"

"In person."

"How in the world did you obtain—"

"The wherewithal to buy it? My godmother left me some pieces of eight. Not a frightful lot, but enough to finance the venture. So now you know why I don't give a hoot for Shoesmith. In a month or so I shall have at least ten thousand quid laid up among my souvenirs. Molloy guarantees this. Shoesmith means less than nothing to me, and that goes for Shoesmith, Shoesmith and Shoesmith. Odd," mused Freddie, "the labels these solicitors' firms stick on themselves. I met a chap in a pub the other day who told me he worked for Hogg, Hogg, Simpson, Bevan, Murgatroyd and Merryweather, and when I said, 'Oh, yes? And how are they all?' he said they expired in the eighties, and the concern now was run by a fellow named Smith. I mean, it just shows how you never can tell, doesn't it?"

A distinct change for the better had come over Lord Blicester's demeanor. It would be too much, perhaps, to say that even now he was all sweetness and light, but he had ceased to eye Freddie as if the latter had been someone with bubonic plague whom he had caught in the act of picking his pocket. The difference between the way an uncle looks at a nephew who has lost his job and whom there is a danger of his having to support and the way he looks at a nephew who has large holdings in a fabulously rich oil company is always subtle but well marked. Some indication of his altered outlook can be gathered from the fact that, though a thrifty man who seldom failed to watch the pennies, he asked Freddie if he would like a liqueur brandy with his coffee. He winced a little when Freddie said he would, for liqueur brandies cost money, but he continued amiable. The peer of the realm, who had been absorbing the proceedings with the goggle-eyed stare with which forty years ago he had watched silent motion pictures, realized that the drama was over and returned to his *truite bleu*.

"Well, I am bound to say this puts a different aspect on the matter," said Lord Blicester. "If you are a man of substance, you naturally do not wish to go on working for a small salary in Shoesmith's office, especially as you are bent on going to Kenya. You think you will like Kenya?"

"My pal Boddington speaks highly of it. The spaces are very great and open there, he tells me."

"There is money, no doubt, in coffee growing."

"Pots, I imagine. I know for a fact that Boddington smokes seven-and-sixpenny cigars."

"Yes, on the whole I think you are doing wisely. Not that I would care to go to Kenya myself."

"I know what you mean. Always the risk, of course, of getting eaten by a lion, which would be a nuisance, but one must expect a bit of give-and-take. I've given the thing a lot of thought, Uncle Rodney, and I'm convinced that Kenya's the place for me, always provided . . ." Freddie paused, and a faint blush mantled his cheek. "Always provided," he went on, "that Sally is by my side. I don't think I ever mentioned this to you, but I'm hoping to get married."

Lord Blicester gave a horrified gasp. Both in physique and mental outlook he was one of London's stoutest bachelors, and he never ceased to think gratefully of the guardian angel who had arranged a breaking-off of relations when years ago he had contemplated marrying Leila Yorke, née Bessie Binns.

"Are you engaged?" he asked anxiously. He was not particularly fond of Freddie, but one has one's human instincts, and he would have experienced concern for anyone on the brink of matrimony.

"That," said Freddie, "we shall know more certainly when Miss Yorke returns. Strictly in confidence, there has been something in the nature of a rift between self and betrothed."

"Ah!" said Lord Blicester, brightening, as a man will who feels that there is still hope.

"And Miss Yorke has gone to phone her and try to talk her round. The trouble was, you see, that when Sally popped in and found this woman in my pajamas— Ah, there she is," said Freddie, rising like a salmon in the spawning season. What, he was asking himself, would the verdict be?

Leila Yorke had the best of news.

"All set," she said briefly, as she reached the table. "You may carry on, Widgeon."

"You mean . . . ?"

"All's quiet along the Potomac. I've made your path straight. You can go ahead as planned. She's ordering the trousseau."

Lord Blicester was trembling a little.

"Do I understand you to say that this girl, whoever she is, is resolved to marry Frederick?"

"The moment he gets the license."

"Good God!" said Lord Blicester, as if he had heard a well-known Harley Street physician telling him that his nephew had but a month to live. He turned to Freddie, agitated. "Did you put anything in writing?"

"Lots."

"Specifically mentioning marriage?"

"Every other line."

"Waiter," Lord Blicester cried, reckless of the fact that Barribault's Hotel charged for this beverage as if it were liquid platinum, "bring me a brandy."

Freddie, though dizzy with relief, did not forget the courtesy due a woman standing by a luncheon table.

"Aren't you going to sit down?" he said.

"I haven't time."

"The day's yet young."

"I daresay, but I've just made a date with my hairdresser, and he can only take me if I get there in ten seconds flat. Thanks for the lunch, Rodney. Fine seeing you again. Just like the old days."

Lord Blicester shivered. He always did when reminded of the old days. But for the grace of God and the sterling staff work of that guardian angel, he was thinking, he would himself have been in his nephew Frederick's frightful predicament.

Leila Yorke had started to move away, but now, as if some basilisk had laid a spell upon her, she halted, rigid, her eyes narrowing. She was looking at the table where Soapy Molloy sat, doing himself well at Oofy's expense. Oofy as a rule was chary of spending his money on others, but when a man has let you have a large slice of so rich a melon as Silver River Oil and Refinery, it is almost obligatory to entertain him at lunch.

She drew a deep breath.

"I suppose one would be put on Barribault's black list if one were to throw a roll at a fellow customer," she said wistfully. "But it's a sore temptation. Look at the low, hornswoggling hound digging into the rich foods like a starving python. Not a thing on his conscience, you'd say.

If I weren't a poor weak woman, I'd step over and push his face in whatever it is he's gorging himself with."

Freddie was not abreast. To what hornswoggling hound, he asked, did she allude?

"Third table down, next to the man with the eyeglass. Fellow with a high forehead."

"You don't mean Thomas G. Molloy?"

"I don't know what his name is. I only met him twice, and we didn't exchange cards. The first time was at Le Touquet, when he swindled me out of a thousand pounds for some shares in a dud oil stock called Silver River, the second when he came to Castlewood one morning and I took a shotgun to him."

Freddie's bewilderment increased. His senses told him that she had applied the adjective "dud" to Silver River Oil and Refinery, but he could not believe that he had heard aright. Nor could Lord Blicester, who had come out of his thoughts and was staring with bulging eyes.

"What did you say?" Lord Blicester cried.

"I was speaking of this smooth confidence man and his Silver River oil stock, and how he talked me into buying it."

"But Silver River is enormously valuable!"

"I don't know who to, except somebody who's making a collection of waste paper. You'd be lucky if you got two-pence a share for it. I know, because I tried and found there was no market. The only offer I got was from a man who had a mentally arrested child. He said he thought the colors it was printed in would entertain the little fellow. And the maddening part of it is that I can't have the bounder arrested, because I made inquiries and found that there actually is a Silver River concern. It's in Arizona somewhere, and he bought it for fifty dollars, it having been worked out to the last drop in 1926. That lets him out and leaves him free to sell shares to innocent mugs like me without getting jugged for obtaining money under false pretenses. Just shows what a world this is," said Leila Yorke, and went off to keep her appointment at her beauty parlor.

She left an uncle and a nephew who looked as if they had been carved out of stone by a sculptor commissioned by a group of friends and admirers to make statues of them. The peer of the realm, who had finished his *truite bleu* and was starting in on a jam omelet, got the impression, as his gaze rested on them, that they must have been eating something that had disagreed with them. Not oysters, for the month was June, and not the *truite bleu,* for that had been excellent. More probably something in the nature of Hungarian goulash, always a dish to be avoided unless you had had the forethought to have it analyzed by a competent analytical chemist.

Lord Blicester was the first to move, and few who had only watched him waddling across the floor in his club smoking room to the table where the papers and magazines were, to get the current issue of the *Sketch* or *Tatler,* would have credited him with the ability to achieve such a turn of speed. In the manner in which he covered the space that separated him from Soapy there was a suggestion of a traveler by the railroad who, with his train due to leave in five minutes, dashes into the refreshment room at Victoria or Waterloo station for a gin and tonic.

Towering over Soapy, he placed a heavy hand on his shoulder and said, "You infernal crook!"

Soapy, whom the words had interrupted at a moment when he was swallowing a mouthful of filet steak medium rare, did not reply, for he was too fully occupied with choking. It was Oofy who undertook the role of straight man, so necessary on these occasions.

"What did you call him?"

"A crook."

"A *crook?* What do you mean?"

"I'll tell you what I mean. That Silver River stock he sold me isn't worth the price of waste paper. The man's a deliberate swindler."

Oofy's jaw dropped. His face paled beneath its pimples. "Are you serious?"

It was a question to which the accepted answer would have been "I was never more serious in my life," but Lord Blicester was beyond speech. His recent sprint had taken its toll. He merely nodded.

The nod was enough for Oofy. Where the other had obtained his information, he did not know, but not for an instant did he question its accuracy. Solid citizens like Lord Blicester do not make scenes in public places unless they have good grounds for them, and in Soapy's empurpled face he seemed to read obvious signs of guilt. Actually, Soapy had turned purple because of the piece of filet steak to which allusion was made earlier, but Oofy was not aware of this. The way he reasoned was that if a man is called a swindler and immediately becomes the color of a ripe plum, the verdict is in, and remembering that in his guest's wallet was a check for two thousand pounds, signed "A. Prosser," he acted promptly. Edging around the table, he flung himself on Soapy and in next to no time had begun to try to throttle him.

There are, no doubt, restaurants where behavior of this sort would have been greeted with a sympathetic chuckle or, at worst, by a mere raising of the eyebrows, but that of Barribault's Hotel was not one of them. Waiters looked at each other with a wild surmise, headwaiters pursed their lips, the peer of the realm said, "Most extraordinary!" and a bus boy was sent out to summon a police-man.

And in due season there arrived not one but two members of the force, and as each of the pair was built on the lines of Freddie's cousin George, they had no dif-ficulty in intervening in time to save a human life, though Oofy, if asked, would have questioned the application of the adjective to the man on whose chest he was now seated. Taking Oofy into custody, they withdrew, and Barribault's restaurant settled back into its normal refined peace.

Freddie saw none of these things. He was sitting at his table with his head between his hands.

20.

It is unusual nowadays for people on receipt of good news to say "Tra-la," though it was apparently done a good deal in earlier times, and Sally, coming away from the telephone at the conclusion of her conversation with her employer, did not actually express herself in this manner. But she was unquestionably in a frame of mind to have done so, for her spirits had soared and life, a short while before as black and dreary as a wet Sunday in a northern manufacturing town, had become once again a thing of joy and sunshine, fully justifying the toast Leila Yorke had drunk to its originator. The word "Whoopee" perhaps best sums up her feelings.

But after happiness came remorse. She shuddered as she

recalled the unworthy suspicions she had entertained of a Frederick Widgeon who, as it now appeared, was about as close a thing to a stainless knight, on the order of Sir Galahad or someone of that sort, as you would be likely to find in a month of Sundays. She should have realized, she told herself, that anyone with a cousin like Freddie's cousin George was practically certain sooner or later to find pajama-clad blondes in his living room. With George at the helm and directing the proceedings, one was surprised that there had not been more of them.

Remorse was followed by gratitude to Leila Yorke for handling the role of intermediary so capably. It was she who, as she always made a point of doing in the novels she wrote, had brought about the happy ending, and it seemed to Sally that some gesture in return was called for. The only thing she could think of was to substitute an extra-special dinner for the chops and fried potatoes she had been contemplating. Putting on her hat, she went out in quest of the materials.

Valley Fields, though more flowers are grown and more lawns rolled there than in any other suburb south of the Thames, is a little short on luxury shops where the makings for a really breath-taking dinner can be procured. For these you have to go as far afield as Brixton, and it was thither that Sally made her way. It was not, accordingly, for some considerable time that she returned. When she did, she found Mr. Cornelius standing on the front steps of Castlewood.

"Oh, Miss Foster," said Mr. Cornelius, "here you are at last. I have been ringing and ringing."

"I'm sorry," said Sally. "I was shopping in Brixton, and my native bearer lost the way, coming home. Is something the matter? Nothing wrong with you, I hope?"

"Not with myself. I am in excellent health, thank you

very much. I always am," said Mr. Cornelius, who had a tendency to become communicative when the subject of his physical condition was broached, "except for an occasional twinge of rheumatism if the weather is damp. No, it is Mr. Widgeon who is causing me anxiety. He is sitting under the tree in the garden of Peacehaven, groaning."

"Groaning?"

"I assure you. I had gone to look at my rabbits, one of whom refused its lettuce this morning, a most unusual thing for it to do, for it is generally an exceptionally hearty eater, and I saw him there. I said, 'Good afternoon, Mr. Widgeon,' and he looked up and groaned at me."

"Didn't you ask him why?"

"I did not like to. I assumed that he had had bad news of some kind, and on these occasions it is always more tactful to refrain from questioning."

An idea occurred to Sally.

"You're sure he wasn't singing?"

"Quite sure. I have heard him sing, and the sound is quite different."

"Well, thank you very much for telling me, Mr. Cornelius," said Sally. "I'll go and see what's the matter."

She hurried into the house, deposited her supplies in the kitchen and went out into the garden. A theory which might cover the facts was forming itself in her mind. Freddie, she had learned from Leila Yorke in their telephone conversation, had been lunching at Barribault's Hotel at his Uncle Rodney's expense, and she knew that when young men accustomed to a cup of coffee and a sandwich at midday find themselves enjoying a free meal at a place like Barribault's, they have a tendency, in their desire to get theirs while the getting is good, to overdo things a little. As she reached the fence, she was hoping that a couple of digestive tablets taken in a glass of water would be enough to bring the roses back to her loved one's cheeks.

The hope died as she saw him. He had risen from his seat beneath the tree and had begun to pace the lawn, and one glance at his haggard face told her that this was no mere matter of a passing disturbance of the gastric mucosa. Even at long range it is easy to discern the difference between a man with an overwrought soul and one who is simply wishing that he had avoided the lobster Newburg at lunch.

"Freddie!" she cried, and he dragged himself to the fence and gazed at her over it with a lackluster eye.

"Oh, hullo," he said hollowly, and with a pang she saw that the sight of her and the fact that after that interlude of icy aloofness she was once more speaking to him had done nothing to lighten his gloom.

"Freddie, *darling!*" she wailed. It seemed inconceivable to her that he had not been informed that his story, fishy though, as her employer had rightly said, it was, had passed the censor. "Didn't she tell you that everything was all right?"

"Eh? Who?"

"Leila Yorke."

"Oh, ah, yes. She told me, and naturally it bucked me up like a weekend at bracing Bognor Regis. The relief was stupendous. That part of it was fine."

"Then what are you looking so miserable about?"

He brooded in silence for a moment. His aspect would have reminded a Shakespearean student, had one been present, of the less rollicking of the Hamlets he had seen on the stage at the Old Vic and Stratford.

"I wish I could break it to you gently."

"Break what?"

"This frightful thing that's happened."

"You're making my flesh creep."

"It'll creep a dashed sight more when you've heard the facts," said Freddie with a certain moody satisfaction. A man with bad news to tell takes a melancholy pleasure in the knowledge that it is front-page news. "I'm sunk!"

"What!"

"Ruined. Done for. I've had it."

"What do you mean?"

"Hang on to your hat while I tell you. You know that Silver River stock of mine?"

"Of course."

"It's no good."

"But I thought—"

"So did I. That's where I made my bloomer. That louse Molloy has turned out to be a hound of the first water. The fiend in human shape is a low-down swindler who goes about seeking whom he may devour. He devoured me all right. A thousand quid gone, just like that, for a wad of paper that would have been costly at twopence. Oh, by the way," said Freddie, remembering, "I've lost my job."

"Oh, Freddie!"

"Shoesmith drove me out into the snow this morning. One darned thing after another, what?"

Sally clung weakly to the fence. Freddie, as she stared at him, seemed to be flickering. Not that it made him look any better.

"The only bright spot is that he gave me a month's salary in lieu of notice, so I'll be able to take you out to dinner tonight. Okay with you?"

Sally nodded. She felt unable to speak.

"It'll be something saved from the wreck. We'll go to the Ritz, and blow the expense. We've still got each other. About all," said Freddie somberly, "we have got."

Sally found speech. "But what are you going to do?"

"Well, that's rather a moot point, isn't it? What *can* I do? Try for another job, I suppose. But as what? We Widgeons are pretty hard to place."

"You can't go to Kenya now?"

"Not if I don't raise three thousand pounds in the next day or two, and the chances of that seem fairly slim, unless I borrow a pickax and break into the vaults of the Bank of England. I had another letter from Boddington yesterday, saying he couldn't keep the thing open indefinitely and if I didn't want to sit in, he'd have to get someone else. No, it looks as if Kenya were off."

Sally started. A thought had occurred to her.

"Unless . . ."

"Unless what?"

"I was thinking of Leila Yorke."

"What about Leila Yorke?"

"Couldn't you get the money from her?"

Freddie stared.

"From Ma Yorke?"

"Yes."

"Three thousand of the best and brightest?"

"It would seem nothing to her. She's got more than she knows what to do with. Everything she writes sells millions of copies, and that last book of hers was sold to the movies for three hundred thousand dollars."

It would be idle to pretend that Freddie's mouth did not water at the mention of such a sum, but he was firm. A Leila Yorke hero, tempted with unclean gold by an international spy, could not have shown a more resolute front.

"No! No, dash it!"

"It would only be a loan. You would pay her back later."

Freddie shook his head. In many ways his ethics in the

matter of floating loans were lax, but on some points they could be rigid.

"It can't be done. Uncle Rodney, yes. Oofy Prosser, quite. If either of them showed the slightest willingness to co-operate and meet me halfway, I would bite his ear blithely. But nick the bankroll of a woman I've only known about a couple of days? Sorry, no. The shot's not on the board. The Widgeons have their self-respect."

And a lot of good it does them, Sally would have said, had she been capable of commenting on this nobility. With part of her mind she was in sympathy with the stern, strong, uncompromising man who had uttered these, she had to admit, admirable sentiments. With the other part, she was wishing she could hit him over the head with something solid and drive some sense into him.

A sudden conviction flooded over her that she was about to cry.

"I must go in," she said.

Freddie gaped.

"Go in?"

"Yes."

"But I need you by my side. We've a hundred things to thresh out."

"We can do that later. I've got to start cooking dinner."

"You're dining with me at the Ritz."

"I know, but Leila Yorke has to eat. I've bought her a guinea hen."

Freddie's emotion expressed itself in an overwrought gesture.

"Guinea hens at a moment like this! Well, all right. When will you be through?"

"She likes dining early. I ought to be ready to start at half-past seven."

"Right ho."

"Goodbye till then," said Sally, and she started for the house just in time. The tears were running down her face as she passed through the back door. She was not a girl who cried often, but when she did, she did it thoroughly.

She was in the bathroom, bathing her eyes, when the front doorbell rang. Wearily, for she assumed that this was Mr. Cornelius come seeking the latest news regarding his next-door neighbor's groaning, she went down and opened the door.

It was not Mr. Cornelius who stood on the steps. It was a tall, thin, seedily dressed man of middle age, whose face, though she was certain that she had never seen him before, seemed vaguely familiar. He was carrying a large wicker-work basket.

"Pardon me," he said. "Are you the lady of the house?"

"I'm her secretary."

"Is she at home?"

"I'm afraid not. But she ought to be back soon."

"I'll come in and wait, if I may," said the man. "I've come quite a long way, and I don't want to miss her."

He sidled round Sally in an apologetic, rather crushed way, and entered the living room. He placed the basket on the floor.

"I've brought the snakes," he said.

21.

There is nothing like a good facial and a new hairdo for freshening a woman up, and it was with an invigorating feeling of being at the peak of her form that Leila Yorke left the beauty parlor and started homeward in her car. Both physically and spiritually she was one hundred per cent. The Surreyside suburbs offer very little in the way of picturesque scenery, but they gave her quite a lift as she drove through them. She found much to admire in Clapham Common, and Herne Hill seemed to her particularly attractive.

Hers was a warm and generous nature. She liked everybody she met, except when tried too high by an occasional Thomas G. Molloy, and nothing gave her more pleasure than to ameliorate the lot of those around her. The thought that she had been able to bring the bluebird back into Sally's life was a very stimulating one, for she was extremely fond of her and on principle disapproved of young hearts being sundered, especially in springtime. She was looking forward to seeing the girl's face, now that all those foolish suspicions and misunderstandings, so like the ones in her novels, had been ironed out. Wreathed in smiles it would be, she assumed.

Her assumption was mistaken. Sally was in the front garden of Castlewood when she arrived, but her face, so far from being wreathed in smiles, had a careworn look. It was the look which always comes into the faces of girls who have just left a living room in which a strange man has been taking snakes out of a wickerwork basket, but Leila Yorke did not know this. The conclusion she drew was that there must have been another rift within the lute between the two young hearts in springtime, and for all her benevolence she could not check a twinge of annoyance. More work, she felt. She enjoyed bringing about reconciliations, but there is a limit. The besthearted of women does not like to have to be doing it every five minutes.

She felt her way into the thing cautiously.

"Hullo, Sally."

"Hullo."

"I've had a facial."

"It looks wonderful."

"Not too bad. Widgeon back yet?"

"Oh, yes."

"You've seen him?"

"Yes."

"Everything nice and smooth?"

"Oh, yes."

"Then why," said Leila Yorke, abandoning the cautious approach, "are you looking like a dyspeptic field mouse?"

Sally hesitated. A witness of her employer's emotional reaction to the recent cats, she shrank from informing her that these had now been supplemented by reptiles of which she knew her not to be fond. But there are times when only frankness will serve.

She said, "There's a man in there."

"Where?"

"In the living room."

"What does he want?"

Again Sally hesitated.

"He came in answer to the advertisement."

Leila Yorke's face darkened. She drew her breath in sharply.

"More cats?"

"No, not cats."

"Dogs?"

"No, not dogs."

"Then what?"

Sally braced herself, feeling a little like one of those messengers in Shakespeare's tragedies who bring bad tidings to the reigning monarch and are given cause to regret it.

"I'm afraid it's snakes this time," she said.

She had not erred in supposing that the words would affect her employer painfully. Leila Yorke seemed to swell like a well-dressed balloon. She was thinking hard thoughts of that unknown sinister Molloy, who stopped at nothing to attain his ends, and she was thankful that in J. Sheringham Adair she had an ally who could cope with him. She hoped that Meredith and Schwed, his assistants, were muscular young men who would spare no effort to show the scoundrel Molloy the error of his ways.

"Snakes?" She breathed strongly. "Did you say snakes?"

"He had them in a basket."

"In the living room?"

"They're all over the floor."

"You shouldn't have let him in."

"He went in."

"Well, if you watch closely, you'll see him going out."

The window of the living room opened on the front garden. With something in her deportment of a leopard on the trail, Leila Yorke went to it and looked in. She stooped, peered, and the next moment reeled back as if the sill on which her fingers had rested had been red-hot. Tottering to the front steps, she collapsed on them, staring before her with rounded eyes, and Sally ran to her, full of concern.

"What is it? What's the matter?"

Leila Yorke spoke in a whisper. Her words were hard to catch, but Sally understood her to say that this, whatever it was, was of a nature to beat the band.

"I might have guessed. Who else would have snakes?"

"You mean you know this man?"

"Do I know him!"

Sally gasped. She saw now why the visitor's face had seemed familiar. There were six photographs of him in her employer's bedroom.

"It isn't . . . ?"

"Yes, that's who it is. Looking just the same as ever. Of all the darned things! I want a drink."

"You're feeling faint?"

"I'm feeling as if some hidden hand had scooped out all my insides and removed every fiber of muscle from the lower limbs."

"There's some cooking sherry in the kitchen."

"Lead me to it. Ha!" said Leila Yorke some minutes

later, putting down her glass. "I think that was rat poison, but it's done me a world of good. I feel myself again. Let's go!"

She led the way to the living room, and paused in the doorway.

"Hullo, Joe," she said.

At the moment of her entry, the visitor had taken up one of the snakes with which the room was so liberally provided and was running it pensively through his fingers, like a man whose thoughts were elsewhere. Hearing her voice, he started violently and stood staring, the snake falling from his nerveless grasp.

"Bessie!" he cried.

Now that she was able to examine him more closely, Sally could see the justice in her employer's criticism of him as weak. His was a pleasant, amiable face, the sort of face one likes at first sight, but it was not a strong one. Weakness showed in the mild eyes, the slightly receding chin and the indecisive lines of the mouth. It would, as Leila Yorke had suggested, have had to be a very non-belligerent goose to which this man could have said "Boo!" and Sally found herself wondering, like everybody else on meeting an attractive woman's husband, why she had married him. Wherein lay the powerful spell he exercised on such a dominant character?

She sensibly reminded herself that it is fruitless ever to try to find the answer to a question of this sort. Love, as a thinker once said, is blind, and these things have to be accepted. She supposed that somebody like Rodney, Lord Blicester, would seek in vain for an explanation of why she loved his nephew Freddie.

Joe Bishop was still staring.

"Bessie!" he gasped again, and ran a finger round the

inside of his collar, as he must have done a hundred times when registering agitation on the stage. "Is it you?"

"It's me. Pick up those damned snakes," said Leila Yorke briskly. Sally, who had sometimes wondered what lovers say when meeting after long separation, felt that now she knew. "The same old faces!" said Leila Yorke, eying the reptiles with disfavor. "That one's Clarice, isn't it?"

"Yes, Bessie."

"And Rupert over there?"

"Yes, Bessie."

"Well, pick them up and put them back in their basket. They remind me of your mother. How is your mother, by the way?"

"She passed on last year, Bessie."

"Oh," said Leila Yorke, and it was so obvious that only with difficulty had she checked herself from adding the word "good" that for a moment there was an embarrassing silence. "I'm sorry," she said, breaking it. "You must miss her."

"Yes."

"Well, now you've got me."

Joe Bishop's spaniel eyes widened.

"But, Bessie, you don't want me back?"

"Of course I want you back. I've been pining away to a shadow without you. I've got octopi spreading their tentacles for you all over London. Why didn't you let me know you were hard up?"

"I didn't like to."

"You an extra waiter with half a dozen snakes to support, all wanting their hard-boiled eggs of a morning. It is hard-boiled eggs the beastly reptiles eat, isn't it?"

"Yes, Bessie."

"Runs into money, that. Took all your tips to foot the

191

bill, I should imagine. I do think you might have come to me."

"But, Bessie, I couldn't. We moved in different worlds. I was down and out, and you were rich and famous."

"Rich, yes, but as for famous, make it notorious. There isn't a critic in England who doesn't shudder at the sound of my name."

"I think your books are beautiful."

"Shows your bad taste."

"Do you know something, Bessie? I started to make a play of one of them."

"Which one was that?"

"Heather o' the Hills."

Leila Yorke frowned thoughtfully, a finger to her chin.

"There might be a play in that. How's it coming along?"

"I couldn't go on with it. I hadn't time."

"Well, you'll have plenty of time now. I'm going to take you down to Loose Chippings in my car right away. Five minutes for you to round up your snakes and ten for me to pack a bag, and we're off."

Sally uttered a cry of anguish.

"But the guinea hen!"

"What guinea hen would that be?"

"I was going to cook you one for dinner."

Leila Yorke was firm.

"It would take more than a guinea hen to make me stay another hour in this lazar house. Give it to the cats. There. must be some of them still around. If they don't want it, you eat it."

"I'm dining with Freddie in London."

"Well, that's fine. Then what you do now is trot around to The Nook and tell Cornelius I'm leaving and he's at liberty to sublet Castlewood as soon as he likes. You stay on tonight and tomorrow close the place up and come to Claines with the bags and baggage. All clear?"

"All clear, Colonel."

"Then pick up your feet and get going. If Cornelius wants to know why I'm pulling up stakes, tell him I think this Valley Fields he's so fond of is a pain in the neck and I wouldn't go on living here if the London County Council came and begged me on their bended knees. He'll probably have an apoplectic fit and expire, but what of that? It'll be just one more grave among the hills. Well, Joe," said Leila Yorke, as the door closed behind Sally, "here we are, eh?"

"Yes, Bessie."

"Together again."

"Yes, Bessie."

"Gosh, how I've missed you all these years, Joe. Remember that flat in Prince of Wales's Mansions, Battersea? And now everything's all right. You can't give me anything but love, baby, but that just happens to be all I require. By the way, I hope I'm not taking things too much for granted when I assume that you do love me as of yore? Well, that's fine. I thought I'd better ask. Do you know what we're going to do, Joe? I'm going to take you for a Continental tour, starting in Paris and wandering around from there wherever the fancy takes us."

"Sort of second honeymoon."

"Second, my foot. We never had a first one. I couldn't leave my sob-sistering, and you were out touring the number two towns with some frightful farce or other."

"Mystery drama."

"Was it? Well, whatever it was, we certainly didn't have a honeymoon. It's going to be very different this time. You've never been abroad, have you, Joe?"

"Once, to Dieppe."

"Well, I've nothing against Dieppe. Swell spot. But wait till you see Marvelous Madrid and Lovely Lucerne, not to mention Beautiful Barcelona and Gorgeous Greece. And when we get back, you can start working on that play."

When Sally returned, she found the exodus well under way. Leila Yorke was at the wheel of her car, and her husband was putting her bag and the snake basket on the back seat.

"All set," said Sally. "I told him."

"How did he take it?"

"He seemed stunned. He couldn't grasp the idea of anyone wanting to leave Valley Fields."

Leila Yorke said it took all sorts to make a world and Mr. Cornelius was to be pitied rather than censured, if he was weak in the head, and the car drove off. It was nearing open country, when Joe Bishop uttered an exclamation.

"I believe I forgot to pack Mabel!"

"You talk like an absent-minded trunk murderer. Who's Mabel?"

"You remember Mabel. The green one with the spots."

"Oh, one of those darned snakes. Are you sure?"

"Not sure, but I think so."

"Well, never mind. She'll be company for Molloy," said Leila Yorke.

22.

At Mr. Cornelius's residence, The Nook, that night prevailing conditions were not any too good. A cloud seemed to have settled on the premises, turning what had been a joyous suburban villa equipped with main drainage, company's own water, four bed, two sit and the usual domestic offices into a house of mourning. Somber is the word that springs to the lips.

When Sally, speaking of Mr. Cornelius at the moment when she had informed him of her employer's abrupt departure, had described him as stunned, she had been guilty of no overstatement. The news had shaken him profoundly, dealing a heavy blow to his civic pride. It seemed scarcely credible to him that anyone having the opportunity of living in Valley Fields should wantonly throw that opportunity away. Leila Yorke was, of course, a genius who laid bare the heart of woman as with a scalpel, but even geniuses, he considered, ought to draw the line somewhere. As he sat with Mrs. Cornelius at their evening meal —a rather ghastly repast in which cocoa, kippered herrings and pink blancmange played featured roles—he was still ruffled.

Mrs. Cornelius, too, appeared to have much on her mind. She was a stout, comfortable woman, as a rule not given to strong emotions, but now she was in the grip of one so powerful that the kippered herring trembled as she raised it to her lips. Even Mr. Cornelius, though not an observant man, noticed it, and when later in the proceedings she pushed the pink blancmange away untasted, he knew that the time had come to ask questions. Only a spiritual upheaval on the grand scale could have made her reject what, though it tastes like jellied blotting paper, had always been one of her favorite foods.

"You seem upset, my dear," he said.

A tear stole into Mrs. Cornelius's eye. She gulped. It had been her intention to remain silent till a more suitable moment, but this solicitude was too much for her.

"I'm terribly upset, Percy. I'm simply furious. I hadn't meant to tell you while you were eating, because I know how little it takes to give you indigestion, but I can't keep it in. It's about Mr. Widgeon."

"Oh, yes? He was groaning in the garden, poor fellow."

"So you told me. Well, I've found out why. I was talking to his cousin, the policeman, before you came back from your office, and he told me all about it. That man Molloy!"

"Are you speaking of Mr. Molloy of Castlewood?"

"Yes, I am, and he ought to be Mr. Molloy of Wormwood Scrubs. He's nothing but a common swindler. Mr. Widgeon told his cousin the whole story. He persuaded Mr. Widgeon to put all the money he had into a worthless oil stock, and now Mr. Widgeon is penniless."

"You mean that Silver River of which he spoke so enthusiastically has no value at all?"

"None. And Molloy knew it. He deliberately stole Mr. Widgeon's money, every penny he had in the world."

Mr. Cornelius's brow darkened. His beard wagged censoriously. He was very fond of Freddie.

"I feared this," he said. "I never trusted Molloy. I remember shaking my head when young Widgeon was telling me about his selling him those oil shares. I found it hard to believe that an American businessman would have sacrificed a large financial gain merely because he liked somebody's face. Things look very bad, I'm afraid. Widgeon, I know, needs three thousand pounds to put into some coffee concern in Kenya. He was relying on a substantial increase in the value of these Silver River shares to provide the money."

"And he's engaged to that nice girl, Miss Yorke's secretary. But now of course they won't be able to get married. And you're surprised because I can't eat blancmange. I wonder *you* can."

Mr. Cornelius, who had been punctuating his remarks with liberal segments from his heaped-up plate, lowered his spoon guiltily, and a somewhat embarrassing silence followed. It was broken by the sound of the telephone ringing in the hall. He went to answer it, and came back breathing heavily. Behind his beard his face was stern. He looked like a Druid priest who has discovered schism in his flock.

"That was Molloy," he said. "He wanted to know if there was any chance of Miss Yorke vacating Castlewood, because, if so, he might like to take the house again. I gave him a very short answer."

"I should think so!"

"I told him that Miss Yorke had already left, and he expressed pleasure and said that he would let me know definitely about his plans in a day or two, and then I said that in no circumstances would I even consider his application. 'I know all, Mr. Molloy,' I said. 'Castlewood,' I said, 'is not for such as you.' I then proceeded to tell him just what I thought of him."

"And what did he say?"

"I seemed to catch something that sounded like 'Ah, nerts!' and then he hung up."

"How splendid of you, Percy! I wish I could have heard you."

"I wish you could."

There was a pause.

"I think I'll have a little blancmange, after all," said Mrs. Cornelius.

In holding the view that his denunciation of Soapy had been of a nature calculated to bring the blush of shame to the most hardened cheek, Mr. Cornelius had been perfectly correct. Only once in his life had he expressed himself more forcibly, on the occasion when he had caught the son of the family which had occupied Peacehaven in pre-Widgeon days, a bright lad of some nine summers, shooting with a catapult at his rabbits. But bitter though his words had been, they left Soapy, who had often been denounced by experts, quite unmoved. He was not a man who ever worried much about harsh words or even physical violence. The falling-out with Oofy Prosser at Barribault's restaurant, for instance, had seemed to him so trivial that he had scarcely mentioned it to his wife on his return from lunch. He classed that sort of thing under the heading of occupational risks, and dismissed it from his mind. All that had interested him in the house agent's observations was the statement that Leila Yorke had left Castlewood. Having replaced the receiver, he sat waiting eagerly for Dolly to return and hear the news. Finding herself short of one or two little necessities, she had gone out earlier to do some shopping.

"Baby," he cried, as at long last the door opened, "guess what. Great news!"

Dolly, who had been putting down her purchases, if one may loosely call them that, turned sharply.

"Don't tell me . . . ?"

"Yep!"

"She's gone?"

"Left this evening."

"Who told you?"

"That guy Cornelius. He's just been on the phone."

"So it's official?"

"That's right."

"Gee!" said Dolly with fervor.

She was feeling all the pleasurable emotions of a general who has seen his plan of campaign work out satisfactorily and knows that he will have something good to include in his memoirs.

"I thought those snakes would do it. Only thing I was afraid of was that there mightn't have been an answer to that advert, on account of it isn't everybody that's got snakes. But I thought it was worth trying, and it was. Well, I'd been hoping to take my shoes off and put my feet up and relax awhile, because let me tell you an afternoon's shopping's hard on the dogs and mine feel like they was going to burst, but we've no time for that. Let's go."

"Go? What's the hurry? We've all the time there is now. We've got it made."

As had so often happened in the course of their married life, Dolly found her consort's slowness of comprehension trying. She would have supposed that even Soapy would have seen what the hurry was. But where a less loving wife might have responded with some wounding reference to Dumb Isaacs who must have been dropped on their heads when babies, she merely sighed, counted ten and explained the situation.

"Look," she said. "You know the Yorke dame hired Chimp to find her lost husband. Well, when a woman's got a private eye working on an assignment like that, she don't cut herself off from the latest news bulletins. If she's checking out, she lets him know. She gets on the phone before she starts and says, 'Hey, I'm leaving for the country. Here's my forwarding address.' "

Soapy's jaw fell. As always, he had not thought of that.

"You think she told Chimp she was pulling out?"

"Of course she did. He may be on his way to Castlewood now."

"Gosh!"

"Only I've an idea he'd wait till it was later. These summer evenings there's generally people about in a place like Valley Fields, and Chimp's one of those cautious guys. Still, we don't want to sit around here, chewing the fat. We gotta move."

"I'm ready."

"Me, too. But let's not go off half-cocked. What'll we need? A torch—"

"Why a torch?"

Dolly counted ten again.

"Because when we get to Castlewood, we aren't going to switch on all the lights. On account we don't want to shout out to the neighbors 'Hey! You thought this house was empty, didn't you? Well, that's where you was wrong. The Molloys are here, come to pick up that Prosser ice.' "

"Oh, I see," said Soapy, taking her point. He could generally understand things, if you used short words and spoke slowly.

"So we'll need a torch. And, seeing that quite likely Chimp'll blow in while we're there, it wouldn't hurt," said Dolly, "to take along my blackjack."

Soapy nodded silently, his heart too full for speech. What a helpmeet, he was saying to himself. She thought of everything.

The journey from the metropolis to Valley Fields can be made by train, by omnibus and part of the way by tram, but if you are in a hurry and expense is no object, it is quicker to take a taxi. Soapy and Dolly did this, and were fortunate to get one of the newer and speedier kind, though to their anxious minds the vehicle seemed to be merely strolling. It was a silent ride. Light conversation is impossible at times like this. Only when they reached their destination and Castlewood's dark, deserted aspect heartened them, did either speak.

"Looks like he's not here yet," said Soapy.

"We'll know that better when we've scouted around some."

"How do you mean?"

"Well, if Chimp's come, he'll have broken a window or sump'n, or how could he get in?"

"Oh, I see."

"You go around that side. I'll go this."

They met at the back door.

"All straight my end," said Soapy.

"Same mine. I guess we're in time."

"You had me worried for a moment, baby."

"I wasn't feeling any too good neither myself," said Dolly. "Well, here goes."

Reaching in her dainty bag, she drew out the blackjack and with a firm hand broke the kitchen window. To Soapy, whose nervous system was not at its best, the sound of splintering glass seemed to ring through the silent night like the clashing of a thousand dishes coming apart in the hands of a thousand cooks, and he waited, breathless, for posses of policemen to come charging on the scene with drawn truncheons. But none appeared. Castlewood and its environs were part of Freddie's cousin George's beat that night, and at the moment of their illegal entry that able officer was standing behind a bush in the garden of a house some quarter of a mile distant, enjoying the cigarette to which he had been looking forward for the last two hours. To keep the record straight, he was also thinking tender thoughts of Jennifer Tibbett, his invariable custom when on night duty.

Standing in the kitchen, Dolly switched on her torch.

"I'm going up. Meet me in the living room."

"You taking the torch?"

"Sure I'm taking the torch. I want to see what I'm doing, don't I?"

"I'll bump into something in the dark."

"Well, bump," said Dolly indulgently. "Nobody's stopping you. This is Liberty Hall, as that cop said."

"Don't talk about cops, baby, not at a moment like this," begged Soapy nervously. "It does something to me. And don't be too long upstairs."

On her return, not even the sight of the chamois leather bag dangling from her fingers was able to restore his composure. He eyed it almost absently, his mind on other things.

"Say, look," he said. "Do you suppose this joint is haunted?"

"Shouldn't think so. Why?"

"I heard something."

"Some what sort of thing?"

Soapy searched for the *mot juste*.

"Sounded kind of slithery."

"How do you mean, slithery?"

"Well, slithery, sort of. I was feeling my way in here in the dark, and there was something somewhere making a kind of rustling, slithery noise. Just the sort of noise a ghost would make," said Soapy, speaking as one who knew ghosts and their habits.

"Simply your imagination."

"You think so?"

"Sure. You're all worked up, honey, and you imagine things."

"Well, if you say so," said Soapy dubiously. "It's all this darkness that gets you down. Beats me why a burglar doesn't go off his nut, having to go through this sort of thing night after night. It would reduce me to a nervous wreck. Could I use a drink!"

"Well, there's prob'ly something in the kitchen. Take the torch and go look."

"Won't you mind being alone in the dark, pettie?"

"Who, me? Don't make me laugh! Matter of fact, I guess it 'ud be safe enough to switch the lights on, if we draw the curtains. And I'll open the window a couple of inches at the bottom. Sort of close in here. If you find anything, bring three glasses."

"Three?"

"Just in case Chimp blows in."

"Oughtn't we to be moving out?"

"Not me! I want to see Chimp's face."

To anyone acquainted with Chimp Twist this might have seemed a bizarre, even morbid, desire, but Soapy followed her train of thought. He chuckled.

"He'll be sore!"

"He'll be as sore as all get out. Get moving, sweetie. Let's have some service."

When Soapy returned, bearing glasses and the bottle of champagne which Sally had been at such pains to buy for Leila Yorke's dinner, he found his wife looking thoughtful.

"Shall I tell you something, Soapy?"

"What, honey?"

"There *is* a slithery noise. I heard it. Like you said, sort of rustling. Oh, well, I guess it's just a draft or something."

"Could be," said Soapy, doubtfully, and would have spoken further, but before he could do so speech froze on his lips.

The front doorbell was ringing.

23.

The sound affected both the Molloys unpleasantly, throwing an instant damper on what had looked like a good party. Soapy, surprisingly agile for a man of his build, executed something resembling the *entrechat* to which ballet dancers are so addicted, while Dolly, drawing her breath in with a sharp hiss, sprang to the switch and turned off the lights. They stood congealed in the darkness, and not even a distinct repetition of the slithery sound which had alarmed him a few minutes before was able to divert Soapy's attention from this ringing in the night. He clutched the champagne bottle in a feverish grip.

"What was that?" he gasped.

"What did you think it was?" said Dolly. She spoke with an asperity understandable in the circumstances. No girl cares to be asked foolish questions at a moment when she is trying to make certain that the top of her head has not come off.

"Someone's at the front door."

"Yeah."

"I'll bet it's a cop."

Dolly had shaken off the passing feeling of having been the victim of one of those gas explosions in London street which slay six. She was herself again and, as always when she was herself, was able to reason clearly.

"No, not a cop. Want my guess, I'd say it was Chimp, wanting to find out if there's anyone home before he busts in. It's a thing he'd like to know."

She had guessed correctly. Chimp Twist, as she had said, was a cautious man. He thought ahead and preferred, before making any move, to be sure that there were no pitfalls in his path. Being in a hurry to get to her car and start shaking the dust of Valley Fields from its tires, Leila Yorke had made their telephone conversation a brief one, and in it had not mentioned whether or not she was being accompanied in her exodus by the secretary who had called at his office. It was quite possible that the girl had been left behind to do the packing.

This provided food for thought. Nothing is more embarrassing for a man who has entered an empty house through a broken window and is anxious for privacy than to find, when he has settled in and it is too late to withdraw, that the house is not empty, after all. This is especially so if he knows there to be shotguns on the premises. Soapy had told Chimp all about Leila Yorke's shotgun, and he shrank from being brought in contact with such a weapon, even if only in the hands of a secretary. So he rang the doorbell.

When he had rung it twice and nothing had happened, he felt he might legitimately conclude that all was well. He left the front doorstep and began to sidle round the house, and he was delighted to find that the very first window he came to had been carelessly left a few inches open at the bottom. It obviated the necessity of breaking the glass, a task to which, for his policy was to be as silent as possible and to avoid doing anything to arouse comment and curiosity in the neighbors, he had not been looking forward. To raise the window was with him the work of an instant, to slide over the sill that of another, and, well pleased, he was just saying to himself that this was the life, when a sudden blaze of light dazzled him. It also made him bite his tongue rather painfully and gave him the momentary illusion that he was in Sing Sing, being electrocuted.

The mists cleared away, and he saw Dolly. Her face was wearing the smug expression of a female juvenile delinquent who has just played a successful practical joke on another member of her age group, and her sunny smile, which Soapy admired so much, seemed to gash him like a knife. Not for the first time he was wishing that, if it could be done without incurring any unpleasant after-effects for himself, he could introduce a pinch of some little-known Asiatic poison into this woman's morning cup of coffee or stab her in several vital spots with a dagger of Oriental design. A vision rose before his eyes of Mrs. Thomas G. Molloy, sinking for the third time in some lake or mere and himself, with a sneer on his lips, throwing her an anvil.

It is never easy at times like this to think of the right

thing to say. What Chimp said was, "Oh, there you are," which he himself recognized as weak.

"Yes, we're here," said Dolly. "What are you doing in these parts?"

A lifetime spent in keeping one jump ahead of the law had given Chimp the ability to think quickly and to recover with a minimum of delay from sudden shocks.

"I came here," he said with a good deal of dignity, "to get that ice for Soapy, like I promised him I would."

"Oh, yeah?"

"Yeah."

"You was going to pick it up and hand it over to Soapy?"

"Yeah."

"For ten per cent of the gross?"

"That was the arrangement."

"Sort of a gentlemen's agreement, was there? Well, that's too bad."

"What's too bad?"

"That you should have had all this trouble for nothing. We've got that ice ourselves. It's over there on that table. And," said Dolly, packing a wealth of meaning into her words as she produced her blackjack from its bag and gave it a tentative swing, "you take one step in its direction, and you're going to get the headache of a lifetime."

Observations like this always cause a silence to fall on a conference. If a Foreign Secretary at a meeting of Foreign Secretaries at Geneva were to use such words to another Foreign Secretary, the other Foreign Secretary would for a moment not know what to say. Chimp did not. He fondled his waxed mustache in the manner of a baffled villain in old-time melodrama, and cast an appealing glance at Soapy, as if hoping for support from him. But

Soapy's face showed that he was in full accord with the remarks of the last speaker.

He decided to make an appeal to their better feelings, though long association with the Molloys, Mr. and Mrs., particularly Mrs., should have told him that he was merely chasing rainbows.

"Is this nice?" he asked.

"I like it," Dolly assured him.

"Me too," said Soapy.

"Yessir," said Dolly. "If there's one thing that gives me a warm glow, it's getting my hooks on a chunk of jewelry like this Prosser stuff. Must be worth fifty thousand dollars, wouldn't you say, Soapy?"

"More, pettie."

"Yup, prob'ly more. When we've sold it to our financial associates, I and Soapy thought we'd go to Paris for a while and walk along the Bois de Boulong with an independent air, like the man who broke the bank at Monte Carlo. We can afford it."

Chimp writhed. His fingers fell from his mustache. Usually, when he let them stray over it, he felt heartened, for he loved the unsightly little growth, but now no twiddling of its spiky ends could cheer him. He was blaming himself bitterly for not having had the sense to come to this house earlier, instead of lingering over his dinner. It had all seemed so smooth to him as he sipped his coffee and liqueur, never dreaming that time was of the essence, and now this had happened.

Although it was already abundantly clear to him that if Soapy and his helpmeet had any better feelings, they were in abeyance tonight, he persevered in appealing to them.

"I want a square deal. I'm entitled to my ten per."

"Oh, yeah? Why?"

"Because I'm Soapy's accredited agent, that's why. You coming down here ahead of me and getting the stuff has nothing to do with it. It's like the Yorke dame and her books. Do you suppose if she went and sold one of them herself, she could collar all the dough and not pay her accredited agent his commish? Sure she couldn't. He'd want his. Same here. And there's another thing. It was entirely owing to me that the Yorke dame lit out. She wanted to stay on, said she liked cats and couldn't have too many around the place, but I made her go. I told her there was a dangerous gang trying to get her out of the joint for some reason and she'd look silly if she woke up one night and found her throat cut. So if there's any justice in the world, if you've one spark of fairness in your— What did you call me?"

Dolly, who had called him a chiseling, double-crossing little hydrophobia skunk, repeated her critique.

"I wouldn't let you in on this for so much as a red cent," she said coldly. "Not even if the Archbishop of Canterbury was to come and beg me with tears in his eyes. You know as well as I do that you was planning to slip a quick one over on I and Soapy, and it was only because we got off to a fast start that you didn't do it. Ten per cent, my left eyeball! We'll give you sixpence to buy wax to put on your mustache, but that's our limit."

Chimp drew himself up. He had never really hoped. What you need when trying to soften the heart of a Dolly Molloy is someone next door starting to play some song on the gramophone that reminds her of her childhood. Either that or a good, stout club.

"Okay," he said. "If that's the way you feel, I have nothing more to say. Except this. What's to stop me walking out that door and calling a cop, and telling him I found you here with the Prosser ice?"

"I'll tell you," said Dolly in her obliging way. "The moment you made a move, I'd bean you. Matter of fact," she went on after a moment's thought, "it wouldn't be a bad idea to do it anyways."

"Now, pettie," said Soapy, always the pacifist, "there's no need for rough stuff," and Chimp said No, he liked women to be feminine.

"There'd be the satisfaction," Dolly pointed out. "Every time I see this little horror from outer space, I want to sock him with sump'n, and now seems as good a time as any."

Chimp backed an uneasy step. He had not forgotten the occasion when the butt end of a pistol in this woman's capable hands had connected with the back of his head, and left him knowing no more, as the expression was. The swelling had subsided, but the memory lingered on.

"Hey, listen!" he cried.

But Soapy and Dolly were listening to the slithery sound which had attracted their attention earlier. It had come again, and this time it was no longer a disembodied rustling. A large green snake was making its way across the carpet.

Joe Bishop's misgivings had been well founded. In saying that he had forgotten to pack Mabel, he had not erred. At the moment when he was gathering up his little flock, she had been overlooked, and for some time she had explored her new surroundings, broadening her mental outlook by taking in fresh objects of interest, and finally fallen into a light doze under an armchair. Waking now from this, she had started out on another sight-seeing tour. Dolly's foot engaged her notice, and she made for it at a speed highly creditable to a reptile with no feet, for she had begun to feel a little peckish. The foot might prove edible or it might not—time alone could settle the point—but it seemed to her worth investigation.

In the circles in which she moved Dolly Molloy was universally regarded as a tough baby who kept her chin up and both feet on the ground, and a good deal of envy was felt of Soapy for having acquired a mate on whom a man could rely. But there were weak spots in her armor, and at times she could be as feminine as even Chimp Twist could have wished. At the sight of Mabel all the woman in her awoke, and with a sharp cry she leaped for the sofa, the nearest object of furniture that seemed capable of raising her to an elevation promising temporary security. At the same moment Soapy, who shared her dislike of snakes, took to himself the wings of a dove and soared up to the top of the bookcase. Mabel, a little taken aback, looked from one to the other with a puzzled expression, not quite, as Freddie's cousin George would have said, having got the gist. Nothing like this had ever happened in the days when Herpina the Snake Queen and her supporting cast had come on next to opening at Wigan, Blackpool and other centers of entertainment.

There is, as a brother author of the present historian has pointed out, a tide in the affairs of men which, taken at the flood, leads on to fortune. It is doubtful if Chimp Twist was familiar with the passage, for he confined his reading mainly to paperback thrillers and what are known as scratch sheets, but he acted now as if the words had for years been his constant inspiration. Dolly's bound had been lissome, and that of Soapy still more so, but neither could compare in agility with the one that took him to the table where the chamois leather bag of jewelry lay, and not even Freddie Widgeon and his friend Boddington, with their liking for the open spaces, could have hastened toward them with a greater zest. Not more than a few seconds had elapsed before he was at the front gate of Castlewood, fumbling at the latch.

He had passed through, and was about to proceed to spaces still more open, when something loomed up before him, and he found himself confronting a policeman so large that his bones turned to water and his heart fluttered within him like a caged bird. He was allergic to all policemen, but the last variety he would have wished to encounter at such a moment was the large.

His immediate thought was that he must get rid of the chamois leather bag before this towering rozzer asked him what it was. Reaching behind him, he dropped it over the gate into the Castlewood front garden.

24.

Freddie's cousin George—for the government employee who had manifested himself from the darkness was he—was glad to see Chimp. A chat with something human—even if, like Chimp, only on the border line of the human—was just what he had been needing to break the monotony of his nocturnal footslogging. Walking a beat is a lonely task, and a man cannot be thinking of Jennifer Tibbett all the time.

"Nice evening," he said.

Chimp might have replied that it had been one until this meeting, but the prudent man does not bandy words with the police, so he merely nodded.

"The moon," said George, indicating it.

"Uh-huh," said Chimp, but he spoke without any real enthusiasm. He was, indeed, not giving the conversation his full attention, for his mind was occupied with thoughts of Soapy and Dolly. He could not believe that his departure had passed unnoticed by them, and he knew that ere long they must inevitably come leaping out in pursuit, modeling their movements on those of the well-known Assyrians who came down like a wolf on the fold. Their delay in doing so he attributed correctly to the magnetism of the snake Mabel, but he doubted if any serpent, however powerful its personality, would be able to detain two such single-minded persons for long. The result was that in the matter of moonlight chats he and George had different viewpoints. George liked them, he did not. He wanted to be up and away, to return for the chamois leather bag later, when conditions would be more favorable to the fulfillment of his ends and aims, and he was regarding George in much the same way as the wedding guest regarded the ancient mariner.

Something of his thoughts may have communicated itself to George, for he abandoned the subject of the moon, seeing that it had failed to grip.

"Been calling on Miss Yorke?" he said.

"That's right. Little business matter."

"She's left. Skinned out this evening."

"So that's why nobody answered the bell. Too bad. I came all the way from London to see her."

"You're not a resident of Valley Fields?"

"No."

"In fact, live elsewhere?"

"Yes."

"Still, you are a householder?"

"Oh, sure."

"Then," said George, falling easily into his stride, "you

will doubtless be willing and eager to support a charitable organization which is not only deserving in itself, but is connected with a body of men to whom you will be the first to admit that you owe the safety of your person and the tranquillity of your home. Coming, then, to the point, may I have the pleasure of selling you for yourself and wife—"

"I'm not married."

"—for yourself and some near relative—as it might be a well-loved uncle or a favorite aunt—a brace of the five-bob tickets for the annual Concert in aid of the Policemen's Orphanage, to be held at the Oddfellows Hall in Ogilvy Street next month. There are cheaper seats—one cannot ignore the half-crown and the two-bob—but the five-bobbers are the ones I recommend, for they admit you to the first three rows. If you are in the first three rows, people point you out to their friends as a man of obvious substance, and your prestige soars to a new high. Money well spent," said George, producing two of the five-bobbers from an inside pocket, for he was confident that his eloquence would not have been wasted.

He was right. Chimp Twist shared Dolly's rugged distaste for encouraging the police force and experienced a strong feeling of nausea at the thought of contributing to the upkeep of a bunch of orphans who would probably, when grown to man's estate, become policemen themselves, but he saw no alternative. Refusal would mean being rooted to the spot while this pestilential peeler renewed his sales talk, and if there was a spot to which he was reluctant to be rooted, with Soapy and Dolly due at any moment, it was the piece of stone paving outside the gate of the desirable villa Castlewood. He could not have been called, as Sally had called Leila Yorke, a cheerful giver, but he gave, and George beamed on him as on a public-minded citizen who had done the right and generous thing. He would have his reward, George told him, for only one adjective could be applied to the forthcoming concert, the adjective *slap-up*.

"No pains are being spared to make the evening an outstanding success. If you knew the number of throat pastilles sucked daily in all the local police stations, you would be astounded," said George, and with a courteous word of thanks he moved off in an easterly direction, while Chimp, anxious to be as far away from him as possible, set a westerly course.

He had proceeded some half dozen yards on this, when the door of Castlewood flew open and Dolly and Soapy emerged in the order named. A few moments earlier, observing that Mabel had turned in again under the arm-chair, they had felt at liberty to descend from their respective perches, and the hunt was on. But there was not much hope in their hearts. With the substantial start he had had, Chimp, they both felt, must by now have joined the ranks of those loved ones far away, of whom the hymnal speaks.

Their surprise at seeing him only a short distance down the road was equaled by their elation. No two bloodhounds, even of championship class, could have produced a better turn of speed as they swooped upon him, and George, who was nearing the corner of the street and had started thinking of Jennifer Tibbett again, paused in midstride, one regulation boot poised in the air as if about to crush a beetle. In the hitherto silent night behind him there had broken out what, had it not been that in the decorous purlieus of Valley Fields such things did not happen, he would have diagnosed as a fracas, and for an instant there surged within him the hope that he was about to make the pinch he had yearned for so long. Then he felt that he must have been mistaken. It was, he told himself, merely the breeze sighing in the trees.

But, he asked himself a moment later, did breezes in trees sigh like that? A country-bred man, he had had the opportunity of hearing a good many breezes sigh in trees, but he had never heard one with a Middle Western American accent calling somebody opprobrious names. He turned alertly, and having turned, stood gaping. Just as a gamester who has wagered his luck against a slot machine becomes momentarily spellbound on hitting the jack pot, so was he numbed by the spectacle that met his eyes. A large citizen appeared to be trying to strangle a small citizen, while in their vicinity there hovered a woman of shapely figure who looked as if she would have liked to join in the fray if she could have found room to insert herself. In other words, as clear and inviting an opportunity for a pinch as ever fell to the lot of a zealous constable.

He hurried to the scene of conflict with uplifted heart. This, he was saying to himself, was his finest hour. If he did not actually utter the words "My cup runneth over," he came very close to doing so. The expression he actually used was the one provided by wise high officials for the use of officers in circumstances such as these.

He said, "What's all this?"

It is a question which, if asked when the blood is hot, often goes unanswered. It did so now. Chimp was in no shape for speech, and Soapy was far too preoccupied with the task in hand. Instead of merely strangling his old associate, George noticed that he now appeared to be trying to pull his head off at the roots, and it seemed to him that the time had come to intervene. His method of doing so, in keeping with his character, was simple and direct. Wasting no time on verbal reasoning, he attached himself to the scruff of Soapy's neck, and pulled. There was a rending sound, and Chimp found himself free from that clutching hand, a thing he had begun to feel could never happen again in this world. For a brief moment he stood testing his breathing apparatus to make sure that it was still in working order; then, in pursuance of his policy of putting as great a distance as possible in as short a time as possible between himself and the Molloy family, he vanished into the night at a speed which Freddie Widgeon, racing of a morning to catch the 8:45 train, might have equaled but could never have surpassed.

George, in his patient, stolid way, was trying to get an over-all picture of the events leading up to this welcome break in the monotony of police work in Valley Fields. His original theory, that the large blighter to whose neck he was adhering had snatched the shapely lady's bag and that the small blighter, happening to be passing at the time, had interfered on her behalf, he dismissed. He had not seen much of Chimp, but he had seen enough to convince him that he was not the type that comes to the rescue of damsels in distress. More probably the small blighter—call him the human shrimp—had spoken lightly of a woman's name, and the large blighter, justly incensed, had lost his calm judgment and allowed his feelings to get the better of him.

Well, that was all very well, thought George, and one raised one's helmet in approval of his chivalry and all that, but you can't have fellows, no matter what the excellence of their motives, committing breaches of the peace all over the place, particularly in the presence of policemen who have been dreaming for weeks of making their first arrest. He tightened his grip on Soapy's neck, and with his other hand grasped the latter's wrist, placing himself in a position, should the situation call for it, to tie him in a reefer knot and bring back to him memories of old visits to the osteopath. And it was at this point that Dolly's pent-up emotions found expression.

"You big jug-headed sap!" she cried.

George started. He knew that this was in many ways a not unfair description of himself, for the fact had been impressed upon him both by masters at his school and, later, by superiors in his chosen profession. His sergeant, for one, had always been most frank on the subject. Nevertheless, the outburst surprised him. He peered over Soapy's head at the speaker and was interested to recognize in her an old acquaintance, might he not almost say friend.

"Why, hullo," he said. "You again? You do keep popping up, don't you? Did I hear you call me a jug-headed sap?"

"Yes, you did," rejoined Dolly with heat. "See what you've been and done, you clam. You've gone and allowed that little reptile to make a getaway and he's got something very valuable belonging to I and my husband."

George shook his head.

"You shouldn't have let him have it. Neither a borrower nor a lender be. Shakespeare."

"Plus which, you're giving my husband a crick in the neck."

"Is this your husband?"

"Yes, it is, and I'll thank you to take your fat hands off'n him."

"Release him, do you mean? Set him free?"

"That's what I mean."

Again George shook his head.

"My dear little soul, you don't know what you're asking. Goodness knows I'd do anything in my power to oblige one with whom I have passed such happy moments, but when you suggest releasing this bimbo, I must resolutely decline to co-operate. He was causing a breach of the peace. Very serious matter, that, and one at which we of the force look askance."

"Oh, applesauce!"

"I beg your pardon?"

"Why all this fuss and feathers about him choking an undersized little weasel that would have been choked at birth if his parents had had an ounce more sense than a billiard ball?"

George appreciated her point, but though as gallant a man as ever donned a uniform he could not allow her to sway him from his purpose.

"I get the idea, of course, and I'd fall in with your wishes like a shot, were the circumstances different, but you're overlooking a vitally important point. Have you any conception of what it means to a rozzer in a place like Valley Fields to be in a position to make a pinch? It's only about once in a blue moon that even so much as a simple drunk-and-disorderly comes along in this super-saintly suburb, so when you get a red-hot case of assault and battery . . ."

Words failed George, and he substituted action. Increasing the pressure on Soapy's neck, he propelled him along the road. Dolly, following, had fallen into a thoughtful silence and made no reply when George begged her to take the sporting view and to bear in mind how greatly all this was going to improve his relations with his sergeant. She was feeling in her bag for her blackjack, a girl's best friend. Experience had taught her that there was very little in this world that a blackjack could not cure.

Chimp Twist, meanwhile, his first instinct being to keep going and get away, had wandered far afield, so far that when at length he paused and felt it would be safe to return to Castlewood and its chamois leather bag, he became aware that he had lost himself. Valley Fields, while not an African jungle, is, like most London suburbs, an easy place for the explorer to get lost in, consisting as it does of streets of houses all looking exactly alike. But much may be accomplished by making inquiries of friendly natives, and after an hour or so of taking the first turn to the left and the second to the right and finding himself back where he had started, he won through to the railway station, and, from there to Castlewood was but a step. His spirits were high as he entered Mulberry Grove, but they became abruptly lowered when he came in sight of the house he sought.

It was not that the sight of the front gate brought back thoughts of George and the Molloys. What caused him to halt suddenly and to realize that Fate was still persecuting him was the spectacle of a young man and a girl standing at that gate, engaged in earnest conversation.

He turned away, with sinking heart. He knew what happened when young men and girls stood in earnest conversation on any given spot. They stayed fixed to it for hours.

25.

Freddie's dinner had been a great success. It had started, as was natural in the circumstances, in an atmosphere of some depression, and during the soup course it would not be too much to say that gloom had reigned. But with the fish there had come a marked change for the better, for it was then that Sally, using all her feminine persuasiveness, had prevailed on him to forget the self-respect of the Widgeons and agree to allow her to apply to Leila Yorke for a temporary loan. After that, everything had gone with a swing.

It was only as they stood at the gate of Castlewood that the jarring note crept back into their conversation. For some little time during the homeward journey Sally had noticed a tendency toward silence on her loved one's part, and now he revealed that, having thought things over a bit, he was not easy in his mind about this idea of appealing for help to Leila Yorke. His scruples had risen to the surface again.

"What I mean to say," he said, "can a Widgeon bite a woman's ear?"

"Oh, Freddie!"

"You can say 'Oh, Freddie!' till the cows come home, but the question still remains moot. Odd, this feeling one has about getting into the ribs of the other sex. It's like rubbing velvet the wrong way. I remember when I was a kid and went to dancing school, there was a child called Alice who had a bar of milk chocolate, and knowing how deep her love for me was I deliberately played on her affection to get half of it off her. I enjoyed it at the time, but now, looking back, I feel unclean. A thoroughly dirty trick I consider it, and I'm not sure this idea of sharing the wealth with Leila Yorke isn't just as bad."

"You won't be getting the money from her. I will."

"But I shall be getting it from you."

"Well, what's wrong with that?"

"Nothing actually *wrong*, but—"

Sally's patience gave out.

"Look here," she said, "do you want to marry me?"

"You betcher."

"Do you want to go to Kenya and make an enormous fortune, growing coffee?"

"Oh, rather."

"And do you realize that you can't do either of these things unless you get some money quick?"

"Yes, I see that."

"Then don't be an ass," said Sally.

Freddie saw her point. He nodded. Her clear feminine reasoning had convinced him.

"I see what you mean. After all, as you say, it's just a loan."

"Exactly."

"Once the coffee beans start sprouting, I shall be able to repay her a thousandfold."

"Of course."

"And you think she'll part?"

"I'm sure she will. She's the most generous person on earth."

"Well, I hope you're right, because I told you about that letter from Boddington, saying he couldn't hold his offer open much longer. The sands are running out, as you might say. You'll be seeing her tomorrow, I take it?"

"Yes, she told me to hire a car and drive down with the luggage. That shows you what she's like. Any other woman would have made me go by train."

"A sterling soul. I've always thought so. She—"

Freddie broke off. Out of the night a large figure in policeman's uniform had appeared and was standing beside them, breathing rather stertorously, as if it had recently passed through some testing spiritual experience.

"Hullo, Freddie," it said.

"Hullo, George."

"Hullo, Miss . . . I keep forgetting your name."

"Foster. But think of me as Sally."

"Right ho. I say," said George, "I've just been conked on the base of the skull with a blunt instrument."

"What!"

"Squarely on the base of the skull. And, what makes it even more bitter, it was a woman who did it. You remember that girl friend of yours who borrowed your pajamas, Freddie?"

"She wasn't my girl friend!"

George was in no mood to split straws.

"Well, your distant acquaintance or whatever she was. Hers was the hand that let me have it."

Sally squeaked incredulously.

"You mean Mrs. *Molloy* hit you?"

"Feel the bump, if you care to."

Freddie drew in his breath sharply. Since his betrothal to Sally, his views on dallying with the female sex, once broad-minded to the point of laxity, had become austere. He spoke severely.

"You have only yourself to blame, George. How you can do this sort of thing beats me. You are engaged to a sweet girl who loves and trusts you, and yet you go about the place forcing your attentions on other women, a thing which Sally knows I wouldn't do on a bet. You ought to be ashamed of yourself."

"What are you talking about?"

"Didn't you kiss Mrs. Molloy?"

"Certainly not. I wouldn't kiss her with a ten-foot pole."

"Then why did she sock you?"

"I was pinching her husband."

A thrill ran through Freddie's system. Anyone who pinched the hellhound Molloy had his sympathy and support.

"I found him causing a breach of the peace, and took him into custody, and we all marched off en route for the police station. The female Molloy had been pleading with me piteously to let the blighter go, and I might have done it, in spite of the fact that it was my dearest wish to make my first pinch and be fawned on by my sergeant and others, but it suddenly came home to me that she had kept referring to the accused as her husband, and I knew she was Mrs. Molloy, and I put two and two together and realized that this must be the bird who had done you down over those oil shares. After that, of course, I was adamant, and the upshot of the whole thing was that while my attention was riveted on Molloy, she hauled off and biffed me on the occipital bone with what I assumed to be a cosh. I don't know what girls are coming to these days."

Freddie clicked his tongue.

"So you let Molloy get away?"

"How do you mean, *let* him get away?" said George, with spirit. "I was temporarily a spent force. Everything went black, and when I came out of the ether I was sitting in the gutter with a lump on the back of my bean— you may feel it, if you wish—the size of an ostrich egg, and the Molloys had vanished into the night."

Sally squeaked again, this time in sympathy.

"You poor man! Does it hurt?"

"Lady, I will conceal nothing from you. It hurts like hell."

"Come on in and have a drink."

George shook his head, and a sharp yelp of pain showed how speedily he had regretted the rash act.

"Thanks, but sorry, no, afraid impossible. I'm on duty, and they have a nasty habit at headquarters of sniffing at one's breath. What I stopped for was to touch you for a cigarette, Freddie. Have you the makings?"

"Of course. I've also got a cigar, rather a good one, judging from the price."

"A cigar would be terrific," said George gratefully. "Add a match—I used my last one just before the affair Molloy—and I shall be set." And having expressed a wish that at some point in his patrolling he might once more encounter Mr. Molloy, he, too, vanished into the night.

His departure left a silence. Freddie broke it.

"Poor old George!"

"My heart bleeds for him."

"Mine, too. Must be very galling for an old Oxford boxing blue, who may at any moment represent his country on the football field, to be put on the canvas by a woman and not to be able to wash it down with a drop of the right stuff. That suggestion of a nip of something to keep the cold out, by the way, strikes me as sound. Have you anything on the premises?"

"I've a whole bottle of champagne I bought for Leila Yorke's dinner."

"You may lead me to it."

They went into the house, and Sally passed on into the kitchen. When she joined Freddie some moments later in the living room, her face was a little pale.

"It isn't there," she said.

"No, it's here," said Freddie, pointing. "Wonder who brought it in? Three glasses, too. Odd."

"I'll tell you something odder. The kitchen window's broken. Somebody's been getting in."

"Burglars? Good heavens!" A grave look came into Freddie's face. "I don't like this."

"I don't like it myself."

"But what on earth would burglars want, breaking into a house of this sort?"

"Well, they evidently did, and what I'm asking myself is, Are they coming back?"

"You mustn't get the wind up."

"I'm jolly well going to. If you want to know how nervous anyone can be, watch me. I've got to sleep here all alone, and if you think that's a pleasant thought, with burglars popping in and out all the time, you're wrong."

Freddie waved a reassuring hand.

"Have no concern whatsoever. I shall be outside, keeping watch and something. Ward, that's the word I wanted. I'll be in the offing, keeping watch and ward. Don't let burglars weigh on your mind. I will be about their bed and about their board, spying out all their ways."

"No, you mustn't."

"Yes, I must."

"No. You need your sleep. I shall be all right," said Sally with sudden confidence. She had just remembered Leila Yorke's shotgun. There is nothing like a shotgun for putting heart into a girl.

Freddie pondered.

"You don't want me to keep watch and ward?"

"No. You're not to."

"Right ho," said Freddie agreeably. Though still a bachelor, he knew better than to argue with a woman. He kissed Sally fondly and left by the front door, and Chimp Twist, who had stolen cautiously to the gate and was about to open it, backed hastily and melted into the night again, thinking hard thoughts of the younger generation. The trouble with the younger generation, he was feeling bitterly as he removed himself, was that they were always round and about, popping up all the time where they were not wanted.

It was perhaps an hour later that he thought it would be safe to try again. He knew exactly where the chamois leather bag was, just behind where he had been standing, and it was with a bright anticipation of the happy ending that he approached the gate once more, only to find the same member of the younger generation leaning on it, his eyes raised to the moon and his general aspect that of one who was there for the night.

A man experienced in dealing with the female sex knows that the policy to pursue, when a woman issues an order, is not to stand arguing but to acquiesce and then go off and disobey it, and Freddie had wasted no time trying to persuade Sally to change her mind and allow him to patrol the grounds of Castlewood. He had simply gone and done it. For the last hour he had been, in defiance of her wishes, walking round and round the house like the better type of watchdog, his eye alert for nocturnal marauders. The complete absence of these had induced ennui and, like George, he was delighted to see Chimp. He would have preferred to pass the time of night with someone who looked a little less like something absent without leave from the monkey house at the zoo, but he knew that he was in no position to pick and choose. Valley Fields goes to bed early, and this at such an hour was the best it could provide.

"Nice evening," he said, though evening was hardly the right word.

Chimp wondered glumly how many people were going to make this quite untrue statement to him. Of all the evenings in his experience, not excluding the one in the course of which Mrs. Thomas G. Molloy had hit him with the butt end of a pistol, this had been the worst. His response to the observation was merely a grunt, and Freddie felt a little discouraged. Here, evidently, was no sparkling conversationalist who would enliven his vigil with shafts of wit and a fund of good stories.

However, he persevered.

"The moon," he said, indicating it precisely as George had done, with a movement of the hand designed to convey the impression that he thought well of it.

It was possible—not probable, perhaps, but still possible—that Chimp would have had something good to say about the moon, but it did not pass his lips, for at this moment, quite unexpectedly, the world came to an end. That, at least, was how it sounded both to Freddie and his companion. Actually what had occurred was that Sally, leaning out of an upper window, had discharged Leila Yorke's shotgun. For the last hour she had been listening in alarm to the sound of stealthy footsteps going round and round the house, and the sight of the two sinister figures standing plotting together at the front gate, evidently exchanging ideas as to how best to sneak in and loot the premises, had decided her to act. The shotgun was in Leila Yorke's bedroom. She proceeded thither, and having found it, took it to her own room, opened the window and pulled the trigger, aiming in the general direction of the moon, for she was a tenderhearted girl and averse to shedding even burglarious blood.

The effect on Freddie and friend was immediate. Chimp, able to understand now why Soapy disliked shotguns, after the first moment of paralysis which so often follows shots in the night, did not linger but was off the mark like a racing greyhound. George, who was enjoying his cigar in the front garden of Peacehaven, keeping his ear to the ground in case his sergeant happened along, got an impression of a vague shape whizzing by, and assumed it to be a flying saucer or something of that nature. Then, like the splendid fellow he was, he remembered that he was an officer of the peace and answering the call of duty hurried in the direction from which the shot had seemed to proceed. At the same moment Mr. Cornelius emerged from The Nook in a beige dressing gown and said, "What was that?" George said that that was precisely what was puzzling him, and Mr. Cornelius said that this sort of thing was most unusual for Valley Fields. They made their way to Castlewood together.

Freddie also was keeping his ear to the ground, and all the rest of him as well. This was because at the moment of the explosion he had flung himself to earth, remembering from Westerns he had seen that this was the thing to do on these occasions. He lay there breathing softly through the nose, and as he lay he became aware of something hard and knobbly pressing into his chest and rendering his position one of extreme discomfort. Cautiously, for when one is under fire the slightest movement is often fatal, he felt for it and pulled it from beneath him. It seemed to be a bag of some description, and appeared to be full of a number of hard substances. He had just slipped it into his pocket and was finding himself much more comfortable when George and Mr. Cornelius arrived. Emboldened by these reinforcements, he rose and accompanied them to the front door, which George banged with his truncheon.

A voice spoke from above.

"Go away, or I'll shoot again. Police!" added the voice, changing the subject. "Police!"

"We are the police, old thing," said Freddie. "At least, George is. For heaven's sake return that damned gun to store and come down and let us in."

"Oh, is that you, Freddie?"

"It is."

"Was that you I saw lying on the ground?"

"It was."

"What were you doing there?"

"Well, commending my soul to God, mostly."

"I mean, why weren't you in bed?"

"I was keeping ward and watch."

"I told you not to."

"I know, but I thought I'd better."

"Oh?"

In the brief interval of waiting for the door to open, Mr. Cornelius enlarged on his previous statement that episodes of this nature were far from customary in the suburb he loved. Not that remarkable things did not happen from time to time in Valley Fields, he added, instancing the case of a Mr. Edwin Phillimore of The Firs at the corner of Buller Street and Myrtle Avenue, who in the previous summer had been bitten by a guinea pig. He was beginning what promised to be a rather long story about a resident named Walkinshaw who came back from London in a new tweed suit and, the animal being temporarily misled by the garment's unaccustomed smell, was chased by his dog onto the roof of his summerhouse, when Sally appeared. She was carrying the shotgun, just in case. She had had an enthralling conversation with someone purporting to be Freddie, but burglars are cunning and know how to imitate voices. They are notorious for it.

George was the first to speak.

"I say, you know! I mean to say, what?" he said, and Mr. Cornelius said, "Just so."

Sally saw their point.

"I know, but you can't blame me. I thought Freddie was one of the gang of burglars who have been in and out of here all night. I'm so sorry I woke you up, Mr. Cornelius."

"Not at all, Miss Foster, not at all. Actually, I was not asleep. I was downstairs, working on my history of Valley Fields."

"Oh, I'm so glad. How's it going?"

"Quite satisfactorily, thank you, though slowly. There is so much material."

"Well, you got some more tonight, didn't you? How's the head, George?"

"Better, thanks."

"But still throbbing?"

"A bit."

"You'd better have that drink, even if you are on duty."

"I think you're right."

"I've got a bottle of champagne."

"My God!"

"It's all ready in there. Freddie!"

"Hullo?"

"You're covered with dust. Come here and let me brush you. What on earth," said Sally, wringing her fingers, "have you got in your pocket?"

"Oh, this?" said Freddie, taking it out. "It seems to be a bag of sorts. I came down on it when I took my purler."

"What's inside it?"

"I don't know. Take a look, shall I? Well, Lord love a duck!" said Freddie. "Well, blow me tight! Well, I'll be a son of a whatnot!"

He was fully justified in speaking thus. From the table on to which he had decanted the bag's contents there gleamed up at them a macédoine of rings, both diamond and ruby, bracelets set with the same precious stones, and, standing out from the rest in its magnificence, an emerald necklace.

George, again, was the first to speak. The police, trained for emergencies, pull themselves together more quickly at times like this than the more emotional householder.

"The bounders dropped their swag!" he said, and Mr. Cornelius, unable to utter, endorsed the theory with a waggle of his beard.

Sally could not accept it.

"But those aren't Leila Yorke's. She hasn't any jewelry except a couple of rings."

"Are you sure?"

"She told me so."

"Then where on earth did the ruddy things come from?" said George, baffled.

A strange light was shining in Freddie's eyes. He had

taken up the necklace and was subjecting it to a close scrutiny. It made all things clear to him.

"I'll tell you where they came from," he said. "From *chez* Oofy. This is the Prosser bijouterie. And if you're going to ask me how I know, I've seen this horse collar on the neck of Myrtle P., née Shoesmith, a dozen times when I've been dining at their residence. She slaps it on even if there is only a Widgeon in the audience. Do you know what this means, Sally? It means that we've come to the end of the long, long trail, and our financial problems are solved. Tomorrow, bright and early, I seek Oofy out and, having restored the stuff to him and been thanked brokenly, I collect the huge reward he'll be only too delighted to bestow. It ought to run into thousands."

It is never easy to find the right words at a moment like this, but George did it. The police are wonderful.

"Open that champagne!" said George.

26.

Feeding his rabbits in the garden of The Nook, Mr. Cornelius, as he plied the lettuce, began to hum one of the catchier melodies from *Hymns Ancient and Modern* and would have sung it, had not the words escaped his memory. He was in the best of spirits. The events of the previous night had left him in a gentle glow, not unlike the one he got from cocoa, kippered herrings and pink blancmange. A kindly man, he wished all his neighbors well, particularly his next-door neighbor, Frederick Widgeon, for whom he had always felt a paternal fondness, and the thought that Freddie's troubles were now at an end, his prosperity assured, the joy bells as good as ringing and nothing for his friends to worry about except the choosing of the fish slicer for a wedding present, was a very heartening one.

A shadow fell on the grass beside him, and he looked up.

"Ah, Mr. Widgeon," he said. "Good evening."

Ever eager to catch the historian in a blunder, carpers and cavilers, of whom there are far too many about these days, will seize gleefully on that word "evening." Did not the historian, they will ask, state that it was in the morning that Mr. Cornelius fed his rabbits? To which, with a quiet smile, the historian replies, "Yes, he did, but this big-hearted animal lover also gave them a second snack around about five p.m., feeling that only thus could they keep their strength up." There was no stint at The Nook.

Mr. Cornelius was glad to see Freddie. A theory concerning last night's happenings had come to him, and he was anxious to impart it.

"I have been thinking a great deal, Mr. Widgeon, about the mystery of how Mrs. Prosser's jewelry came to be in the front garden of Castlewood, and I have come to the conclusion that under a mask of apparent respectability the man Molloy must have been one of these Master Criminals of whom one reads, a branch of his activities being the receiving of stolen goods. He was what I believe, though I should have to apply to your cousin for confirmation, is known as a fence."

"Oh, no, quite all right," said Freddie.

"I beg your pardon?"

"You said something about taking offense."

Mr. Cornelius was concerned. He saw that his companion's eyes were blank, his manner preoccupied. He had learned from Sally, with whom he had had a brief conversation as she was preparing to drive off to Claines Hall in her hired car, that Freddie had set out for London in the morning to restore the stolen jewelry to its owner and be lavishly rewarded by him, and he would have expected to see him on his return wreathed in smiles and feeling, as he had once described it, like one sitting on top of the world with a rainbow round his shoulder. Yet here he was, manifestly a prey to gloom. Exchanging glances with the rabbit nearest to him, he was frowning at it as he had frowned at the Texas millionaire in the restaurant of Barribault's Hotel.

"Are you feeling quite well, Mr. Widgeon?"

Dotted throughout this chronicle there have been references to occasions when Freddie Widgeon uttered mirthless laughs, but on none of these had he produced one comparable for lack of jollity with that which now passed his lips. It was a mirthless laugh to end all mirthless laughs, and sounded like a gramophone needle slipping from the groove.

"No," he replied, "I'm not. I'm feeling the way George must have felt last night when beaned by that cosh of Mrs. Molloy's. Do you know what, Cornelius?"

Mr. Cornelius said he did not.

"You don't know Oofy Prosser, do you?"

"We have never met. I have heard you speak of him, of course."

"Well, if you ever do meet him, you will be doing me a personal favor if you sit on his chest and skin him with a blunt knife. The louse has done me down."

"I don't understand."

"I went to see him this morning."

"So Miss Foster told me."

"Oh, did you see Sally? She got away all right?"

"Yes, I saw her off in her car. She had a snake with her, belonging, I understand, to Miss Yorke's husband. She was taking it to Claines Hall. It is a curious story. It appears— But you were telling me about your visit to Mr. Prosser."

Freddie raised a protesting hand.

"Don't call him Mr. Prosser, call him the hound Prosser or the Prosser disease. I went to his house in Eaton Square, and found him in sullen mood. He had just come from Bosher Street police court, where the presiding magistrate had soaked him for a fine of ten quid, telling him he was pretty dashed lucky not to have got fourteen days without the option."

"You astound me, Mr. Widgeon! Why was that?"

"Didn't I tell you he tried to murder Molloy at Barribault's yesterday? No? Well, he did, and the gendarmerie scooped him in and he spent last night in a prison cell. He was pretty sore about it, what embittered him chiefly being the fact that he was given a bath by the authorities. He wouldn't talk about anything else for the first ten minutes, but when I could get a word in edgeways, I handed him the bijouterie, and he said, 'What's this?' I explained that it was his better half's missing jewelry and said that, while I would not presume to dictate and would leave the matter of the reward entirely to him, I thought ten per cent of the value of the gewgaws would be fair to all parties concerned, and what do you think his reply was? He said he would be blowed if he gave me a ruddy penny, adding that if a few fatheaded buttinskys like me were to refrain from being so damned officious and weren't always meddling in other people's affairs, the world would be a better and sweeter place. It seems that he insured the stuff for about twice its proper value and got the money, and now he would have to give it back to the insurance people. He was very heated about it, so, seeing that my presence was not welcome, I came away. And I'd been counting on getting my three thousand quid from him," said Freddie brokenly, still gazing at the rabbit, but now as if seeking its sympathy.

He received none from that quarter, rabbits being notoriously indifferent to human suffering—lettuce, lettuce, lettuce, that is all that ever matters to them—but he got plenty from Mr. Cornelius. The house agent's beard quivered, as a bearded man's beard always will at the tale of a friend's distress. He became silent, seeming to be pondering on something or trying to come to some decision. At length he spoke.

"There *is* another source from which you can obtain the money you require, Mr. Widgeon," he said.

Freddie was surprised.

"Oh, did Sally tell you about her idea of trying to get the necessary funds from Leila Yorke? It looks like being our last chance, now that Oofy has declined to do the square thing. I phoned her from the Drones about Oofy letting me down, and though of course knocked slightly base over apex by the news, she speedily rallied and said everything was going to be all right, because she was sure that Leila Yorke would come through, she having a heart of gold and more cash than you could shake a stick at. Well, I wore the mask and said, 'Oh, fine!' or words to that effect, but I don't mind telling you, Cornelius, that I'm far from happy at the thought of letting a woman pick up the check. It jars my sense of what is fitting. True, as Sally keeps pointing out, it's merely a loan and it isn't as though she were kissing the stuff goodbye. Nevertheless—"

He would have spoken further, but at this moment a bell sounded, and he drew the fact to his companion's attention. A man of the other's age might well be hard of hearing.

"Your phone's ringing, Cornelius."

"Yours, I think, Mr. Widgeon."

"By jove, so it is," said Freddie, starting into life. "It must be Sally. Excuse me."

Left alone, Mr. Cornelius fell into a reverie. Rabbits twitched their noses at him, at a loss to understand why there had been this unexpected stoppage in the hitherto smoothly running lettuce supply, but he remained plunged in thought, not heeding their silent appeal. Minutes passed, and when at length Freddie came out of the back door of Peacehaven, a glance told Mr. Cornelius that he had not received good news. His aspect reminded the house agent of his brother Charles at the time when there was all that trouble about the missing cash from his employer's till. Charles, confronted with the evidence of his peculations, had looked as if something heavy had fallen on him from a considerable height, and so did Freddie.

Wasting no time on preambles, he said, "Well, that's torn it!"

"I beg your pardon?"

"I'm sunk!"

Again Mr. Cornelius begged his pardon, and Freddie forced himself to a semblance of calm. In order to get the sympathy he was seeking, he saw that he must be coherent.

"That was Sally on the phone, speaking from Claines Hall, Loose Chippings, and what do you think she told me? Leila Yorke has gone!"

"Dead?" said Mr. Cornelius, paling.

"Worse," said Freddie. "Legged it abroad with her husband on a sight-seeing jaunt, leaving no address but just a note saying that they were going to roam hither and thither about the Continent in the car, she didn't know where, and she didn't know when she would be back. In short, she has disappeared into the void, breaking contact with the human herd, and can't be located. You see what that means?"

"You will be unable now to apply to her for assistance in your financial emergency?"

"Exactly. I would have said that now we haven't an earthly way of touching her, but your way of putting it is just as good. And I have to give Boddington my decision in the next couple of days or so. Now you see why I said I was sunk. I see no ray of hope on the horizon."

It was stated earlier in this chronicle that the luxuriant growth of Mr. Cornelius's beard rendered it hard for the observer to see when he was pursing his lips. A similar difficulty presented itself when he smiled, as he was doing now. Freddie may have noticed a faint fluttering of the foliage, but nothing more. He continued in the same lugubrious strain.

"Leila Yorke was my last hope. Where else can I raise the needful?"

"Why, from me, Mr. Widgeon. I shall be delighted to lend you the money, if you will accept it. That was what I meant just now, when I spoke of an alternative source."

Freddie stared.

"You?"

"Certainly. It will be a pleasure."

There came to Freddie the feeling he had sometimes had when trying to solve a *Times* crossword puzzle, that his reason was tottering on its throne. There was nothing in the other's appearance to indicate that he had gone off his rocker, and still less to suggest that he was trying to be funny, but he could place no other interpretation on his words.

"Listen," he said. "Are you sure you've got this straight? It isn't a fiver till Wednesday week that I want, it's three thousand pounds."

"So I have always understood you to say."

"You mean you've actually *got* three thousand pounds?"

"Precisely."

"And you're willing to lend them to me?"

"There is nothing I would like better."

"But look here," said Freddie, his scruples troubling him again. "I'll admit that these doubloons would mean everything to me, and it's a great temptation to sit in on the project, because I honestly believe from what Boddington tells me that I should be able to pay you back in the course of time, but I don't like the idea of you risking all your life's savings like this."

Once more, Mr. Cornelius's beard stirred as if a passing breeze had ruffled it.

"These are not my life savings, Mr. Widgeon. I think I have spoken to you of my brother Charles?"

"The one who's living in America?"

"The one who was living in America," corrected Mr. Cornelius. "He passed away a few days ago. He fell out of his airplane."

"I'm sorry."

"I also. I was very fond of Charles, and he of me. He frequently urged me to give up my business and come and join him in New York, but it would have meant leaving Valley Fields, and I always declined. The reason I have brought his name up in the conversation is that he left me his entire fortune, amounting, the lawyers tell me, to between three and four million dollars."

"What!"

"So they say."

"Well, fry me for an onion!"

"The will is not yet probated, but the lawyers are in a position to advance me any sums I may require, however large, so you can rest assured that there will be no difficulty over a trivial demand like three thousand pounds."

"Trivial?"

"A mere bagatelle. So you see that I can well afford to lend you a helping hand, and, as I told you before, it will be a pleasure."

Freddie drew a deep breath. Mr. Cornelius, his rabbits and the garden of The Nook seemed to him to be executing a spirited version of the dance, so popular in the twenties, known as the shimmy.

"Cornelius," he said, "you would probably object if I kissed you, so I won't, but may I say . . . No, words fail me. My gosh, you're wonderful! You've saved two human lives from the soup, and you can quote me as stating this, that if ever an angel in human shape . . . No, as I said, words fail me."

Mr. Cornelius, who had been smiling—at least, so thought Freddie, for his beard had been in a constant state of agitation—became grave.

"There is just one thing, Mr. Widgeon. You must not mention a word of this to anyone, except of course Miss Foster, in whom you will naturally have to confide. But you must swear her to secrecy."

"I'll see that her lips are sealed all right. But why?"

"This must never reach Mrs. Cornelius's ears."

"Hasn't it?"

"Fortunately, no."

"You mean she doesn't know? You haven't told her about these pennies from heaven?"

"I have not, and I do not intend to. Mr. Widgeon," said Mr. Cornelius, graver than ever, "have you any conception of what would happen, were my wife to learn that I was a millionaire? Do you think I should be allowed to go on living in Valley Fields, the place I love, and continue to be a house agent, the work I love? Do you suppose I should be permitted to keep my old friends, like Mr. Wrenn of San Rafael, with whom I play chess on Saturdays, and feed rabbits in my shirt sleeves? No, I should be whisked off to a flat in Mayfair, I should have to spend long months in the south of France, a butler would be engaged and I should have to dress for dinner every night. I should have to join a London club, take a box at the opera, learn to play polo," said Mr. Cornelius, allowing his morbid fancy to run away with him a little. "The best of women are not proof against sudden wealth. Mrs. Cornelius is perfectly happy and contented in the surroundings to which she has always been accustomed—she was a Miss Bulstrode of Happy Haven at the time of our marriage—and I intend that she shall remain happy and contented."

Freddie nodded.

"I see what you mean. All that program you were outlining sounds like heaven to me, but I can understand that you might not get the same angle. Just depends how you look at these things. Well, rest assured that none shall ever learn your secret from Frederick Fotheringay Widgeon, or, for the matter of that, from the future Mrs. F. F. W. Her lips, as I say, shall be sealed, if necessary with Scotch Tape. I wonder if you'd mind if I left you for a space? I want to go and phone her the good news."

"Not at all."

"I won't be able to see it, but her little face'll light up like glorious Technicolor. Thanks to you."

"My dear Mr. Widgeon, please!"

"I repeat, thanks to you. And if ever there's anything I can do for you in return—"

"I can think of nothing. Ah, yes. Could you tell me how 'Rock of Ages' goes?"

"A horse? I don't think I have it on my betting list."

"The hymn."

"Oh, the hymn? Now I get your drift. Why, surely, tum tumty tumty tumty tum, doesn't it?"

"The words, I mean."

"Oh, the words? Sorry, I've forgotten, though I seem to recall the word 'cleft.' Or am I thinking of some other hymn?"

Mr. Cornelius's face lit up, as Sally's was so shortly to do.

"Why, of course. It all comes back to me."

"Well, that's fine. Anything further?"

"No, thank you."

"Then for the nonce, my dear old multimillionaire, pip-pip."

Freddie hurried into the house. Mr. Cornelius returned to his rabbits, who were feeling that it was about time.

"Oh, rock of ages, cleft for me," he sang.

The rabbits winced a little. They disapproved of the modern craze for music with meals.

Still, the lettuce was good, they felt philosophically. A rabbit learns to take the rough with the smooth.

P. G. WODEHOUSE *was born in Guildford, England, in 1881 and educated at Dulwich College, a school in the suburbs of London. He worked in the Hong Kong and Shanghai Bank for two years and then got a job writing a column in the* Globe. *He came to America in 1909 and has lived in the United States the greater portion of the time since. He has written over sixty books, as well as magazine serials and short stories beyond count. He has also been a highly successful collaborator on musical shows with Guy Bolton and Jerome Kern. It would be hard to name another writer whose work has held up steadily at top caliber over so long a period.*

Mr. Wodehouse is an Honorary D.Litt. of Oxford University. He became an American citizen a few years ago. He and his wife live the year round in Remsenburg, Long Island.